Alcott is the best school in the city and tough on every kid who goes there, but Sam Davidson bears what's got to be the ultimate burden—his father is the school's headmaster. Sam's "over-privileged" status subjects him to all kinds of pressures both in school and at home, but his protests to his father fall on deaf ears. With no hope of transferring to another school, Sam follows his natural bent for being a class clown. To the Alcott teachers his name spells trouble in capital letters. But there is far more serious trouble at Alcott that the teachers, and the headmaster, know nothing about. Someone is extorting money from middle-school kids and even from fourth graders. When the trouble does begin to surface it is Sam who is accused—there are certain members of the Alcott faculty all too willing to believe that Sam is guilty—and what Sam knows he cannot tell.

NAT HENTOFF is a well-known writer who is on the staff of *The New Yorker* and is a regular contributor to *The Village Voice, Playboy, Atlantic Monthly,* and *The New York Times.* He is the author of *Jazz Country* and *I'm Really Dragged But Nothing Gets Me Down* (the latter available in a Laurel-Leaf edition).

THE LAUREL-LEAF LIBRARY brings together under a single imprint outstanding works of fiction and nonfiction particularly suitable for young adult readers both in and out of the classroom. The series is under the editorship of Charles F. Reasoner, Professor of Elementary Education, New York University.

This School Is Driving Me Crazy

A NOVEL BY

NAT HENTOFF

Published by
Dell Publishing Co., Inc.
1 Dag Hammarskjold Plaza
New York, New York 10017

Laurel-Leaf Library ® TM 766734, Dell Publishing Co., Inc.

ISBN: 0-440-98702-4

Reprinted by arrangement with Dealcorte Press.
Printed in the United States of America
First Laurel-Leaf printing—February 1978
Second Laurel-Leaf printing—July 1978

For this book's first readers,
who kept me keeping on—
Nicholas, Thomas, Jessica, Miranda,
Mara, Lisa, and especially Margot.

1

"There's a kid in one of Benjy's math classes," Sam said as he smeared strawberry jam on a slice of toast and stuck his sleeve in it as he reached for a cup of cocoa with his other hand, "whose father is headmaster of Trafalgar, but his father sends him to *our* school because *his* father says it's not fair for a kid to be in a school where the headmaster is his own father. It's hard on the kid, and it's hard on the father."

"Here," Sam's mother said, handing him a napkin, "after you take that jam off your sleeve, you might reach into your shirt pocket and remove that strip of bacon. Unless you're saving it for a mid-morning snack."

"So why," continued Sam, smearing the jam over a broader area of his sleeve with the napkin, "do I have to go to dad's school?"

"Because your father does not believe in taking the easy way out. And he does feel, you know, that his school is the best in the city. So he doesn't want you, his own son, to go to a lesser school."

Sam took the bacon out of his shirt pocket and ate it. "It's not good for a kid to be overprivileged," he muttered.

"Don't be fresh," his mother said with a smile. "Also, your father thinks he'd be a pretty weak headmaster if he couldn't show that he's capable of treating you just the same as all the other students at Alcott."

"Yeah." Sam finished his cocoa in a gulp. "Sometimes I wonder if he remembers my name."

Suddenly, frantically, he went through his pockets, dived to the floor, looked under the table and under his chair, shot up again, scanned the table, pounced on the bowl of cereal, grabbed his bus pass from inside the bowl and shoved it, wet, into his shirt pocket.

"Still," Sam said, cramming books and notebooks and two pens without their tops into his book bag, "it's a funny feeling when you hear kids swearing at the headmaster and it's your own father they're using words about that you won't let me say at home."

"Don't you stand up for him?" his mother said as she lit a cigarette. Sam lunged at it and she pulled her hand back.

"You said you'd stopped smoking." Sam stood in front of her, looking like a small bull about to paw the earth.

"I am in the process of stopping," his mother said irritably. "Besides, someone who has not learned how

2

to stop *himself* from fighting in school—someone who has to be stood over and yelled at every night so he'll do his homework, *if* he hasn't forgotten it in school—someone who has lost two, *two,* jackets in school in two weeks—someone who—"

"O.K., O.K." Sam stared at the cigarette and then at his mother, drawing a finger across his throat.

"—someone who is wearing, right this minute, one brown shoe and one sneaker, is not the person to be lecturing anyone else about *anything*," his mother went on. "And you did not answer me. Don't you stand up for your father?"

"That," Sam said as he put on his corduroy jacket and stuck a banana in the right-hand pocket, "is just what the kids would like. If I did that, they'd call him even worse names."

"Aren't they afraid you'll tell on them?" His mother was looking at Sam's feet and shaking her head.

"Jees, Mom! What kind of kid do you think I am? They know better than that."

"It is just as well for everyone concerned that your father has breakfast before we do."

"Yeah," Sam nodded. "Like dad says," he went on, making his voice as deep as he could, " 'The head of a school should be the first one in, and the last one out.' " Sam saluted. "Dad thinks he's captain of a ship."

"Watch it now," his mother said, pressing her lips together to suppress a smile. "No disrespect. Now go take that sneaker off!"

"No time," Sam shouted, heading for the door. "The headmaster says, 'A late boy is a lazy boy, and a lazy boy is a loser.' "

Sam's mother rose. "He never said that. Come back here!" she called to Sam's back. "Your father does not allow sneakers in school!"

"No time, no time," Sam yelled. "And anyway, it's not a full pair."

"Sam!" His mother now was yelling, too. "What are you doing with those pumpkins?"

Sam, his book bag around his neck, his bus pass in his teeth, a pumpkin twice as big as his head in one arm, and a second pumpkin in the other, was just barely able to open the door. Leaving it open, he pressed the elevator button with his nose, saw the elevator was going up past his floor, and walked slowly over to the stairs. Once on the street, he walked carefully to the bus corner and waited, hunched over, with his book bag nearly touching the ground. As his bus pulled up, he sighed with relief and slowly, ever so carefully, went up the stairs and leaned over the change box toward the bus driver.

"Fare, young man," the driver said.

"Bssss pssss." Sam's face was now very close to the driver's.

"Hey now," the driver said as he drew back. "What is this? I'm not a relative of yours."

In despair, Sam opened his mouth, letting the bus pass fall at his feet.

"The bus pass." Sam nodded anxiously toward the floor while just managing to keep the pumpkin in his left arm from falling. But that motion loosened his grip on the other pumpkin, which landed on the driver's lap.

"I had my bus pass in my teeth," Sam explained.

The driver, staring at Sam stonily, lifted the pumpkin from his lap and stuck it under Sam's right arm. "You keep that," he said. "We are not allowed to take food from the passengers."

Slowly, carefully, Sam lowered himself, a pumpkin clutched to each side, until he was close enough to the floor to make a try at getting the bus pass between two fingers. The bus started up, jouncing one of the pumpkins loose. Sam, straightening suddenly to go after the pumpkin rolling down the aisle, banged his elbow against the change box, howled in pain, and howled again on seeing the second pumpkin follow the other to the back of the bus.

"Hey," the bus driver said, "aren't you the kid who had roller skates on yesterday?"

Sam kept his eye on the pumpkins, now stuck in a thicket of passengers' feet. "That was me. I'm not gonna do that anymore. I almost rolled under the bus when I got off."

"O my God!" the driver cried as he stopped short at a red light. "Off! Off! Get those pumpkins and get off this bus. I don't take drunks and I don't take boys who get themselves and everybody else in trouble."

"You can't kick me off," Sam protested. "I have a bus pass."

"I decide who gets on this bus," the driver said and his voice rasped and rose. "And I decide who stays on this bus. Out!"

A large, red-faced man picked up the pumpkins, brought them to the front of the bus, inserted them under Sam's arms, and said to the bus driver, "You're not serious? The boy didn't do anything."

"Yeah," Sam agreed. "I didn't do anything. Show me where it says pumpkins aren't allowed to ride a bus."

"Now look here," the driver said over Sam's head to the large man, "this maniac almost made me cut his legs off yesterday. I want him to learn a lesson. Maybe next time he'll come on the bus without pumpkins, without roller skates, without driving me crazy."

"Now look here yourself"—the large man's face seemed to swell—"you've got no right to throw this kid off. Suppose it was your kid?"

"I don't have any children, thank God." The driver opened the door, and Sam, hugging the pumpkins to his chest, jumped down.

"You don't have to get off, you know," the red-faced man shouted after him.

"That's O.K.," Sam shouted back. "I'll remember his number, and I'll sue him."

"You are not allowed on this bus—*forever!*" The driver was really shouting now.

"And you a grown man," an elderly woman seated just behind the driver spoke accusingly into his ear.

"I have a good mind to order *everybody* off this bus," the driver muttered.

As the bus drove off, Sam frowned, put the pumpkins on the ground, and searched his pockets wildly. "Damn," he said, "I never picked the bus pass off the floor."

Fifteen minutes later, Sam and the two pumpkins, the latter somewhat mashed for having bounced more than a few times on the sidewalk, arrived at the Bronson Alcott School.

At the door, the guard, a short, round black man in his late forties, his mustache trim, his blue uniform crisp, looked at his watch.

"Second time this week," he announced.

"I got thrown off the bus," Sam said. "Once you've paid your fare, the driver's got no right to do that, has he?"

"Not unless you did something terrible," the guard smiled. "And knowing you . . ."

"Oh, come on," Sam said, losing his grip on one of the pumpkins, which hit the ground. "That driver was just prejudiced." Sam kept the remaining pumpkin close to his body as he slowly lowered himself to pick up the other one. "He hates pumpkins."

"Then you better report him to the Great Pumpkin, Charlie Brown," the guard said, laughing.

Not funny, Sam said to himself, moving past the guard, weaving slightly from side to side for balance. Finally, he reached the door of his classroom. As lightly as he could, Sam banged on the door with his forehead. The teacher turned away from the blackboard, saw Sam, sighed, and opened the door.

"How nice of you to come," Miss Sullivan said. "I had already marked you absent."

Sam walked to the back of the room, each head at each desk following his passage, and tenderly placed the pumpkins in a corner.

"Remember?" Sam gestured as grandly as he could toward the pumpkins. "Remember, Miss Sullivan, I said I'd bring the biggest I could find for the Halloween party."

"I do appreciate your keeping your word, Sam, which you always do." Miss Sullivan looked from Sam to the battered pumpkins and could not resist adding, "But did you dribble them to school?"

Over the giggling of the class, Sam said morosely, "I had some problems."

"Your history report, please?" Miss Sullivan held out her hand.

Sam hit himself on the head with his left hand while rummaging through his book bag. Then, with both hands, he attacked his shirt pockets and his jacket pockets. As the banana fell out of his jacket, Sam saw a mental image of the history report back home on the kitchen table, next to the cup of cocoa, and bitterly blamed his mother for not having reminded him to take the damned report with him.

"I see," Miss Sullivan said. "You will report for detention to Mr. McEvoy this afternoon. And if you do not bring in that report tomorrow, you will have to go to the headmaster."

"I know," Sam groaned and sank into his seat.

"And Sam," Miss Sullivan said not unkindly, "I would strongly suggest that tomorrow you leave that sneaker on your left foot home and put on the mate to that brown shoe you have on your right foot."

The class roared. Sam laughed too and stuck the sneakered foot in the air.

"Maybe his feet got a split personality?" someone yelled from the back of the room.

Miss Sullivan smiled, went back to the blackboard and asked, "Now what was the second reason the Indians became hostile to the colonists?"

"The colonists wouldn't let them wear moccasins," Sam volunteered.

"Enough!" Miss Sullivan stared at Sam. "Will you ever learn to quit before you're hopelessly behind?"

2

"You want me to wait around until you finish detention?" Benjy asked Sam late that morning. They were walking toward the lunchroom.

"No, thanks." Sam threw a fake punch at a kid he knew coming the other way. "You never know what Mr. McEvoy's going to do. He may keep me after for one period, or if he hasn't finished reading his newspaper, he may say at the end of one period that I have to stay for two. I just hope he doesn't give me lines to do."

Benjy laughed. "What was that one you had to do two hundred times last week?"

"*Alcott students are always honest. They do not use an expired subway pass. If they have lost this month's bus pass, they pay the fare.* Damn, nobody ever looks at the date if you move fast enough. It's my luck the two kids in front of me sneaked under the turnstile and ran like hell. Then everybody got stopped."

"How come *you* didn't sneak under?" Benjy asked.

"Because it's wrong, that's why," Sam said.

"But you were going to try to beat them for a fare your way," Benjy persisted.

"Say, Benjy," Sam said, ignoring the last comment, "what do you think about school?"

Sam stopped, bent down to tie his sneaker, and looked up at his oldest friend. He couldn't remember when he didn't know Benjy. It was a good thing, Sam was thinking, to be able to go back that far with somebody who wasn't a parent. You had no choice with parents, and they had no choice with you. You're stuck with each other. But if he and Benjy didn't choose, and didn't keep choosing, to like each other, there'd be no reason for them to keep going home from school together and hanging out with each other on the weekends.

"What's to think about?" Benjy looked at Sam curiously. The questions that guy thinks up, Benjy thought. Questions you can't do anything about, so what's the point of asking them?

"Can't you imagine it better?" Sam asked. "Can't you imagine a school you'd *want* to go to?"

"Like, for instance?"

"Like a school," Sam said, "where you'd never have to do anything you didn't want to. If you didn't feel like math, you could read. If you didn't feel like reading, you could play ball."

"Boring," Benjy said.

"What do you mean, boring?"

Benjy pretended to throw up as he looked at the gooey macaroni and cheese that was the day's lunch. "After a while," he said, "you'd get bored doing anything you wanted to. It'd be like summer all year long. I mean, summer's O.K. up to about the first week in August, but then, you know what, I start wanting somebody to tell me what to do even if I don't want to do it."

"The trouble with you," Sam said, "is you haven't got much imagination."

"What the hell does that mean?"

"It means," Sam said, "there's always *something* to do. There's never any *reason* to be bored. Watch.

"MY RETAINER! MY RETAINER!" Sam howled. "I'VE LOST IT!"

"There's nothing wrong with your teeth," Benjy whispered. "You don't *have* a retainer." If Sam wasn't a friend of mine, Benjy was thinking, I'd figure him to be the biggest jerk in creation. And you know what? He is the biggest jerk in creation.

"REWARD! REWARD!" Sam was yelling. "I LOST MY RETAINER, I LOST MY *DEN-TAL* APPLIANCE. IT'S IN THE MACARONI OR SOMEWHERE IN THE ICE CREAM. REWARD! REWARD!"

The food line stopped. Some of the kids already at their tables looked at their trays, grimaced, and pushed them away.

Mr. McEvoy, the head of the middle school, a tall, thin, balding man who prided himself on his ability to remain calm, or at least appear calm, whatever the provocation, walked briskly over to Sam.

"You really did not have to tell the whole world," he said. "Now, are you *sure* you lost your retainer?"

Sam, trying not to grin, nodded affirmatively. Benjy, who had moved several steps away, was looking fixedly at the ceiling.

"Wait a minute," Mr. McEvoy said. "You don't have a retainer! I remember your mother saying that at least your *teeth* are perfect." He began to make noises in his throat.

Jees, Sam thought, Mr. McEvoy sounds like he's growling. He sounds like—like a dog.

"Sam!" Mr. McEvoy's voice was loud, but it sounded strangled. "This is a *joke*, isn't it?"

Benjy moved farther away from Sam, who kept his head down.

"Well," said Sam, "it just came to me, you see, Mr. McEvoy."

The head of the middle school, the growls coming faster and deeper, shut his eyes for a few seconds and then, enunciating each syllable with great care, said, "You already have an appointment for detention with me this afternoon, Sam. It will be a long appointment. And you will have a very long composition to write on why students must not act like baboons in the school cafeteria.

"ALL RIGHT!" Mr. McEvoy tried to make his voice carry throughout the cafeteria. "ALL RIGHT! NO RETAINER, NO DENTAL APPLIANCE FELL INTO ANY OF THE FOOD. ONE SMALL BOY THOUGHT HE WAS BEING *FUN-NY*. HE WAS NOT BEING *FUN-NY*. AND HE IS GOING TO BE VERY SAD. CONTINUE YOUR LUNCH!"

The kids at the tables looked suspiciously at their food trays, and some began to poke around in the macaroni. The food line started moving again, but most of the kids, judging by how little macaroni they took, didn't seem to be very hungry.

"Terrific," Benjy said to Sam. "Terrific. If that's what you call imagination, I'd rather have a toothache."

"What was that all about?" asked Blake Edwards, who had been waiting in the food line. "You crazy?" he said to Sam.

"Some days nobody's got a sense of humor," Sam said, annoyed at Benjy and annoyed at himself.

"Now, look here." Blake poked Sam in the chest. "Food is nothing to fool around with. Even what they call food here. You can mess with me a whole lot of other ways, but do not mess with my food. First of all, by eleven o'clock, I am not thinking about nothing but food. And second, eating time is the only time you get for yourself in this school the whole damn day. You picked the wrong place, man, to have your joke, if that's what it was."

"Oh, go to hell—both of you!" Sam said. He stalked off.

At the Bronson Alcott School, students on scholarship were presumably known only to the headmaster and to those people in his office who were in charge of such affairs. The headmaster was fond of saying at parents' meetings and during his various lectures on education, "Everyone in this school is judged by merit. I *will* not have our teachers make any assumptions about any member of this student body on the basis of his family being poor. The ability to learn has nothing to do with family income. There are some mighty dumb rich kids and there are some very bright poor kids whose families are on welfare. It is to make sure that no assumptions are made about any child on the basis of his parents' income that we reveal only the percentage of Alcott students on scholarship—and never their names."

"Now isn't that stupid?" Benjy was fond of saying. "Most of the time we can tell who's on scholarship by where they live."

Everybody, for instance, knew that Blake Edwards was on scholarship. They knew it not because he was black. There were black kids at Alcott who lived in immediately identifiable middle-class neighborhoods. But Blake came from so far uptown that even though he had been at Alcott since the second grade, no white Alcott boy had ever visited his home.

Sam had been vigorously instructed by his mother— his father tried to avoid the subject—that Blake's neighborhood was extremely dangerous and that racial prejudice had nothing whatever to do with her ordering Sam, under no condition, to go there.

"That must make Blake feel great," Sam had once said to his father, "going home alone every day. He's an Alcott boy only when he's in school, right?"

"It's an unfortunate situation," the headmaster said, "but it's just not safe where he lives. Not safe for black kids, and especially not safe for white kids. We at the school can't change that situation, and I'm sure Blake realizes it."

Some of the Alcott boys would occasionally invite Blake to their homes after school, but he usually declined. Unless it was Sam or Benjy. "You got to have a couple of friends at school," Blake had told the kids he hung out with uptown, "and those two dudes at least are interesting. They don't come on funny if you're black. Neither funny cold, or funny like they're scared you're going to mug them right there in the middle of the classroom. I mean they're straight-out, you know. Especially that Sam. He doesn't care what he says to anybody. I dig that because I'm like that too."

"But what I don't understand about Sam," Blake was saying to Benjy after he too had decided he wasn't all that hungry for the macaroni and cheese, "is why he does these nutty things."

"That's just Sam," said Benjy as he and Blake headed for their math class. "One summer, when we were both about six, we were at a place on the ocean. That is, the ocean's on one side, and there's a bay on the other. An island, you know. So we were playing around the dock, and a truck comes down the road.

"'Betcha I can stop that truck,' Sam says. I thought he was just talking. All of a sudden, Sam's in the middle of the road, standing there right in front of the truck. The driver's yelling at him and Sam isn't moving. All us kids are watching, and Sam, he keeps shaking his head every time the driver tells him to get the hell out of there. I thought that guy was going to throw Sam right into the bay. What finally happened was, they had to send for his father. He came running down, pulled Sam out of the road, and whacked him hard on the behind. But Sam didn't cry at all. He seemed to enjoy the whole thing."

"Yeah, I've known kids like that," Blake said. "They

come on like they can do *anything,* just ask them. And you don't have to ask them. I knew a dude, little bitty thing he was, who used to invite us to his house and say did we want to talk to the Temptations or the Jackson Five. And he'd call up the record company, even if it was in California, and find out where they were working, and he'd call *there.* None of them ever talked to him, you know, but he was sure a big man with that telephone. Until his mother finally figured out the phone company wasn't making no mistake. She *owed* all that money. That little fellow couldn't sit down—hell, he could hardly move—for a week. And now he looks at a phone like it's going to eat him.

"But he keeps doing other nutty things," Blake went on. "He can be one pain in the ass, but he sure doesn't put you to sleep. You never know what that little fellow's going to do next."

"Yeah," Benjy said, "he sounds like Sam."

"But Sam!" Blake said, shaking his head in wonderment, "he's acting like that, and he's the headmaster's son!"

"Well, how would *you* like to be the headmaster's son," Benjy asked, "and have a father who pretends he's not your father? During the day, anyway."

"That is a strange scene," Blake said. "My own dad drives a cab nights, so I don't hardly see him at all. But I don't know what I'd do if he was running the school I was going to. I think that if I'd been Sam's father, I would have sent him to some other school. It ain't natural this way."

3

"I'll trade you Mel Ott and Johnny Mize for Ted Williams," Sam whispered that afternoon. Miss Saperstein was conjugating a French verb on the board.

"How come?" Fat Jake asked.

"My father grew up in Boston and liked the Red Sox, O.K.? I want to give it to him for his birthday, O.K.?"

"You're making me cry," Jake said. "I want your Tris Speaker and your Ty Cobb, too."

"You are some faggot, you faggot!" Sam snapped.

Jake turned around, fist held high, and whacked Sam on the top of the head. Sam punched Jake in the ear and was about to go for the other ear when Miss Saperstein yelled, "Samuel Davidson! Up front!"

Sam left his seat, poked Jake in the neck as he walked by, drew away before Jake's punch to his stomach could land, and slowly, wearily, walked up to Miss Saperstein's desk.

"What was all that about?" she glared at Sam.

"He's a jerk," Sam said.

"I simply do not understand," Miss Saperstein shook her head, "why it is that whenever there's any trouble in this class, you're at the bottom of it. I tell you, Samuel, we shall have to go to your father as soon as class is over."

"About what?" Sam felt as if he were about to throw up.

"You need help, Samuel. And we're going to arrange for you to get it."

Something, some terrible signal of warning, made Sam turn around just in time to see Jake's hand coming from inside Sam's desk. In that hand was Sam's collection of baseball cards with a rubber band around them.

"Goddamn!" Sam yelled as Jake threw the cards out the window. Sam rushed to the window, climbed halfway out, and saw the packet of cards land in the playground below.

"Stop, Sam, stop!" Miss Saperstein ran for the window and grabbed for Sam who, eluding her grasp, now stood on the ledge, holding tightly to the window sash. "I won't tell your father. I won't," Miss Saperstein was shaking. "I *promise*. Please, please, *don't jump*."

Sam edged a bit farther away from the window without loosening his hold on the sash. "Tell that faggot," Sam said, trying to keep his fright from showing, "to go down there and get my cards and bring them to me. Then I'll come in."

"He's full of it," Jake said to Miss Saperstein. "Let him stay there. He'll crawl in soon enough."

"You little bastard," Miss Saperstein shrieked at Jake. She was really shaking now. "You get the hell down there and bring back those cards. *Fast!*"

Jake, stunned, trying not to cry, did cry. Sobbing, he said, "I'm going to tell my mother what you called me."

"Get those cards!" Miss Saperstein yelled.

Sam, closing his eyes so as not to look down, held on fiercely to the window sash, and started rehearsing for dinner. Dad, it wasn't what she thought. I was just looking to see where those cards had gone, and then, well, then I was just *there,* out on the ledge. I mean, I wasn't going to jump or anything. I'm not crazy. She just got the wrong idea. Anyway, what business did that fat jerk, Jake, have to do that to my cards? It's all *his* fault.

No, Sam sighed inwardly. That won't work. Well, he thought to himself with some satisfaction, at least I'm getting those cards back.

That evening at dinner, Carl Davidson stared at Sam as if he were looking at cream that had gone sour.

"Do you think that looking at you gives me any pleasure?" he said to his son. "I don't mean just today, with a sneaker on one foot and a shoe on the other. It's every day. I don't know how you do it, but your mother swears that when you leave this house in the morning, you're reasonably clean and neat. Well, as neat as you are capable of being. But by the time I see you in school, you look as if you've been shot out of a cannon. O.K., that I find unpleasant aesthetically, but I wouldn't dwell on it if you took care of some of your other responsibilities."

"Can't this wait until after dinner?" Mrs. Davidson asked, passing the melon.

"No, it can't, Liz. This—this yo-yo—is not only falling behind in two subjects. He is not only contemptuous of spelling and paragraphing, whatever the subject. He has not only caused at least one of his teachers to buy a magnifying glass so that she can try to decipher his handwriting—"

"I hadn't heard about that," his wife said.

"I did, today." The headmaster went on, "Miss Sullivan, who is a very decent, conscientious woman, asked me if perhaps Sam had had a hand injury along the way. I told her that he has an acute case of chronic sloppiness. Anyway, in addition to all that, he is the class clown. The class fool. Are you aware," his father turned toward Sam, "that Miss Saperstein was so upset after that dumb stunt of yours that I told her to take the rest of the afternoon off?"

"Yes, Sam," his mother said, "what *possessed* you to do a thing like that?"

Sam looked longingly at the melon. "Well, it just happened. I wanted to make sure where my cards had gone and, I dunno, there I was on the ledge."

"Then why, once you saw where you were," his father said heavily, "didn't you go back into the room instead of frightening the bejeebers out of Miss Saperstein?"

"She got so upset, I just froze," Sam said. "I mean, if she'd only asked me to come in, I would have. But she started yelling about jumping, and I didn't know what was going on."

"That *is* possible, Carl," Mrs. Davidson said. "I understand why she got hysterical, and panic can be catching."

"Liz, the boy does a damn fool thing that could have gotten him killed, and you find excuses for him."

Sam looked at his father. "Listen, I know it was dumb. If you want me to say I'll never do that again, I'll say it because I never will do that again. Just like I won't go on a bus wearing roller skates again."

"Great, that's another one we can check off," his father said. "Now we've only got maybe two million damn fool things you *haven't* done yet."

"Carl," said his wife, "let the boy eat his dinner."

"Go ahead and eat," the headmaster barked. "What I also want to know is when you are going to start shaping up in math and in French, among other subjects."

"You told me not to talk while I'm eating."

"Wise guy," his father said and attacked his melon.

"All right," Sam sighed. "It's what I've told you before. It's what a lot of the kids will tell you. We've hardly got time to breathe at school. It's just like it says in the catalog: 'Students will be involved in supervised activities from the minute they arrive until they depart in the afternoon.' We all know that one by heart. 'The Slave Code' is what the kids in the upper school call it."

Sam leaned forward with the passion of his complaint. "Then each teacher thinks all we're taking is his subject, and every one of them piles it on. It's just not *fair* for a twelve-year-old to have three hours of homework a night."

"It would not have to take three hours," his father said, "if you could ever learn to organize yourself. If you didn't spend the first hour hunting for the assignments and then calling somebody up because you forgot half of them in school. And then listening to the radio in some kind of trance until your mother wakes you out of it. And then finally, maybe, getting down to do some work, and yelling you don't have enough time before you have to go to bed."

"Too much pressure," Sam said.

"Pressure!" His father raised his eyebrows. "*You* give pressure, you put pressure on everybody—your mother, the teachers—"

"Wait, Carl," Mrs. Davidson cautioned as she lit a cigarette. "Maybe he's not academic. At least not yet. Maybe Alcott, good as it is, just isn't the right school for Sam. Sam as he is now."

"Yeah!" Sam agreed enthusiastically, and he banged his spoon on his plate, which cracked.

"Oh, God," his mother said. "Do you have to do *everything* so emphatically?"

"Tell me, dear boy," Sam's father said with exaggerated sarcasm, "what kind of a school would you like to go to?"

"Well," Sam answered seriously, "there's that Free Learning Community School on the West Side. I met some kids from there in the park. They learn what they want to learn in that school. They don't have to take any dopey math or French if they don't want to. Well, they have to take math sooner or later, but it's all done with games. And if they don't feel like sitting in *any* class some days—you know, there are days like that—they can just paint or make something."

"Great," the headmaster said. "Marvelous. The school for fools. Pick out any kid there, ask him for a dollar's worth of change, and he may give you forty-two cents. On a good day, I mean, when what's left of his brain is working. Or ask any kid there what the Magna Charta is, and they'll tell you it's a rock group.

"You listen to me, young man. I am not a fool and you are not going to be a fool. Whether you like it or not, on bad days and on good days, you are going to stay in the toughest and therefore the best school in this city. You are going to organize yourself and you are going to work much harder and you are going to stop acting like a baboon in class."

They all think I'm a monkey, Sam said to himself, remembering how Mr. McEvoy had described him in the lunchroom earlier that day.

"But, dad," he said out loud, "what *sense* does it make to go to a school I hate? I bet if I didn't have all that pressure, I wouldn't get into so much trouble. Sometimes I think I *am* going crazy."

"*You* are the cause of your trouble," his father said as he banged the table and Mrs. Davidson looked at the condition of *his* plate. "As for what you call pressure, the lives of most men who became successful began with a tough, demanding childhood. Tough, not crazy. You're no crazier than I am. You're just a whole lot dumber, and we are going to take care of that."

"There are other ways to be smart than in school." Sam looked down at the table.

"Oh, sure," his father said. "You can be a smart

bum, knowing which hallways you can sleep in when it's cold without getting kicked into the street. You can be a smart forty-five-year-old elevator man, if there are any elevators left that aren't automated by then."

"Funny," Sam said. "Very funny."

"You're right, it isn't funny," his father said sharply. "It wasn't meant to be. Now pay very close attention. You are almost thirteen years old, and it's about time you started growing up."

"I wish I could," Sam said. "I'm the shortest boy in the whole class."

"That is not what I meant by growing up," his father said.

"I didn't think it was," Sam said, reaching for the milk.

Pacing the bedroom floor a few hours later, Carl Davidson stopped in front of the bed. His wife, propped against the pillows, was staring at him.

"*You're* the expert on children," she said. "You're the one who gets seven hundred and fifty dollars each time you speak at those conferences—paid for by God knows whom—on 'What Is Education For?' or 'Standardized Testing: True or False?' or 'Why Johnny Can't Write Two Decent Sentences in a Row and He's Already in Graduate School or—' "

"Or 'Are Schools Obsolete?,' " the headmaster joined in, "and 'Affective Learning: Are We Forgetting the Feeling Child?' There's *one* conference I'd sure like to set up myself. It would be called: 'Stop All the Dancing Around and Teach Them How to Read and How to Understand What They Read.' "

"You've gotten me off the subject, which is Sam," Mrs. Davidson said. "O.K., you're an expert, so what do you do with a boy who teeters on a window ledge outside his classroom, who makes everybody in the lunchroom sick to his stomach, and who gets thrown off a bus—all on the same day?" She laughed. "You know, as I say all these terrible things he does, they don't seem all that terrible. Exasperating, but not mean or really *disturbed*."

"Still," the headmaster said, "there's something missing in that boy. No, not missing, rather not connected. A boy doesn't keep acting like that if he's really together inside. There's something loose in Sam, something that keeps craving attention all the time, every minute, almost every second." The headmaster laughed.

"What's funny?" his wife asked.

"I was thinking of the kind of attention my father would have given me if I'd acted like Sam." The headmaster smiled ruefully.

"Hit you with his belt, I suppose?"

"No. Nothing like that. He would not have spoken to me or in any way acknowledged my presence for at least a week, maybe two weeks. When my father was really fed up with me, he would look through me as if I were air. I remember once when I had called him stupid. I must have been about seven. After a day and a half of being totally ignored, I couldn't stand it anymore and so while he was reading the paper, I jumped on his lap. I figured he'd have to pay attention to me then. Do you know what he did? He got up without saying a word and let me drop to the floor. Now *that's* punishment."

"How awful," Mrs. Davidson said. "Not even you could do that."

"What do you mean, not even I could do that?" he said, genuinely shocked. "My God, you must really think I don't know anything about children. If I acted that way toward Sam, he'd be in the loony bin, or I'd be in the loony bin because of what he'd do *then* to get my attention. Good Lord, you can't say I ignore the boy."

"Well, you don't ignore him when you're *with* him, which is mostly at dinner. You're always on him, as a matter of fact. But right after dinner, you go into your study or you're off to a school meeting or you're lecturing somewhere. Think about it. How much of your time do you actually give up just to be with Sam? Dinner doesn't count. Have you ever taken him to a baseball game or a basketball game?"

"Oh, come on," the headmaster said. "You know what my schedule is like. Evenings, what evenings I have at home, are for reading. And even so, I'm always way behind. I've got to know something about what's inside all these new books—are they ever going to slow down?—on what's wrong with education. I've got to read them so that I can blow holes in them when a parent asks why we're not tightening discipline or when another kind of parent demands that we do this or that to 'humanize' the school. One woman asked me last week why it wasn't possible for us to abolish grades since her child broods when he doesn't get an *A*. I told her to ask him if they keep score in the ballgames he plays."

"That's not a very good analogy," his wife said.

"It was good enough for her. My job isn't to educate parents. I never tell them more than they can understand. Anyway, there are all kinds of other things I have to read—departmental reports, budget committee reports, complaints from parents, complaints from teachers, complaints from seniors about how I'm squelching their spirit because I will not have Meditation or Open Marriage among their elective courses. I also have to keep up with changes in college admissions procedures and I have to deal with all those damn committees the board of trustees sets up. If only trustees would realize they're just good for raising money. The headmaster is supposed to take care of everything else, and if the trustees don't like the way he's running the school, let them get another headmaster. But, in the meantime, they ought to keep the hell out of educational policy. You know what I brought home tonight? A trustees' committee report on how we can save money by dropping our courses in Russian and Chinese. That's *my* decision to make, damn it, and I'm going to tell them so."

"It's a pity," his wife interrupted, "that we can't put report covers around Sam and bind him in. Then you might pay some real attention to him."

"Why the hell are you putting all the blame on me?" The headmaster was pacing again.

"Carl," she said, "you try to get to know something about all the kids at Alcott, right? And you try to get to know a lot more about the kids who are having a bad time at school. So figure it out. You've just told me what happens to your time when you're home. If your evenings are all gone, and much of your weekends too, I might add, what does that leave? It leaves the hours you're in school. And when you're not dealing with the problems adults make for you there, you're thinking about and working with the kids at Alcott, especially the kids who need particular attention. Very concerned attention. So Carl, how much time do you have left for Sam?"

There was no answer.

"I don't mean to make you feel bad," his wife continued. "I'm trying to show you that you're right. Sam is trying to get attention, all the time. He's trying to get your attention."

"Oh, that's too simplistic," her husband said.

"Just think about it." Mrs. Davidson put out the light next to her bed. "If you have time."

"Liz," the headmaster said, "I love that boy."

"I know," she said, "but I'm not all that sure he knows."

4

The next morning, Sam and Benjy decided to take the subway to school. On the subway platform they were suddenly surrounded by six big kids.

"What school you go to?" one of them said, grinning coldly.

"P.S. 68," Sam said quickly. Benjy nodded vigorously.

"That's funny," the kid said. "You look like private-school punks with those blue jackets. Or maybe you're twins, huh?"

"Listen, man." Sam inserted the thumb of his left hand in his belt and made a fist in his right pocket.

"What you got in that pocket?" the older boy said as he and his companions moved closer to Sam and Benjy. "Is that a grapefruit or a stiff dick."

All six of the bigger boys laughed.

"O.K.," their spokesman said, "hand it over. I want all the money both of you got."

Benjy was frantically digging into his shirt pocket when Sam started yelling, "HELP US KIDS! HELP US KIDS! MUGGERS! MUGGERS! PARENTS—HELP US KIDS!"

Three men, including a subway cop, rushed toward the clump of boys.

"You little bastard," the leader of the gang said as he took a swipe at Sam, who ducked. A woman behind them started bashing the older boy in the face with her pocketbook.

"POLICE, MURDER! HELP!" she screamed, battering the gang leader harder with each cry. He twisted away and jumped down onto the tracks as the other members of the gang sprinted up the subway stairs.

"You're a pretty generous kid," said Sam, grinning at Benjy. "Don't give the money until you have to."

"You are out of your mind," Benjy said, breathing heavily. "They could have killed us."

"No way," Sam said. "We're too young to die."

"You've got detention for the whole week?" asked Tim Rawlins, a skinny, fellow sixth-grader. They had met at the entrance to the school that morning and were walking to their first class. He desperately wanted to tell Sam his own troubles, but figured that first he ought to show some interest in Sam's.

"Yeah," Sam said. "Between my going out the window and causing all that macaroni and cheese to go to waste and wearing a sneaker, McEvoy gave me five days, two periods each, and six hundred lines—two hundred for each thing I did bad. That's going to be great for my character, right? To hell with my hand. My hand's going to be permanently crippled. Six hundred lines! Some school! All we need now is a watchtower with guards."

Coming along the corridor toward Sam and Rawlins were Fred Brompton, George Howes, and Bill Maguire, all tenth-graders. Sam had never had any trouble with them, but he knew that Brompton, Howes, and Maguire were bullies and were scrimy besides. "Scrimy" was a special word between Sam, Benjy, and Blake. It meant, among other things, someone who smiles when he's about to bash you by surprise or who swears he wishes he could lend you a quarter and later, you see him take a fistful of change out of his pocket. Most of all, scrimy meant someone grown-ups say you ought to act like but who kids wish would fall down the nearest sewer and never come up. Scrimy Brompton, Howes, and Maguire were always like choirboys when a teacher was around, but Sam didn't trust them for a second.

"You just *know* what some people are like," Sam had once said to Benjy and Blake about Brompton, Howes, and Maguire. "I bet you could have told right away what kind of kids those three were when they were two years old, in the sandbox. They probably grabbed everybody's pails and then kicked them in the face. That goes for Marty Brompton too, that scrimy Fred's big brother. So he's a big deal on the football team. But I've seen him bully little kids."

As Sam and Rawlins were about to pass the three older boys, the younger Brompton laid his hammy hand on Tim Rawlins' shoulder. "See you soon," he said. "Right?"

Biting his lip, Rawlins nodded.

"What's the matter?" Sam asked him as the three older boys moved down the corridor.

"Nothing." Rawlins bit his lip again.

"Say," Sam stopped. "What the hell is going on?"

There were tears in Rawlins' eyes. "Will you promise not to tell anyone?" he asked. "Not your father, not anyone?"

Sam agreed, although he hated making that kind of promise because, once made, it had to be kept, no matter what. It could be like having a big stone inside your chest. Like when he once promised a kid he hardly knew that he wouldn't tell anyone about his mother. They'd gone to the kid's house after school and found the mother so drunk she fell into a closet on the way to get them some cookies. Since that day, the kid had barely spoken to him, and Sam was still carrying around this thing that had nothing to do with him.

Tim Rawlins blinked, gulped, and his voice came out breaking. "They make me give them money."

"Those three horses' asses?"

Rawlins nodded. "A dollar for each of them twice a week. It's been going on for three weeks now. I got my allowance raised to three dollars, and now I tell my mother I need extra money for notebooks and class trips and things. But she's getting suspicious. And this morning—you swear you won't tell anybody about any of this?"

"Yeah," Sam said, looking around to see if anyone was coming. Damn, it's like *I* have something to hide, he thought, feeling sour inside.

"This morning"—Rawlins brought his teeth together

hard to keep the dry heaves down—"I took five dollars from my father's wallet."

"For Christ's sake." Sam exploded. "Turn the bastards in. One thing I know about my father is that he'll kick their asses right out of here."

"No," Rawlins said. "They'll beat the hell out of me if I tell."

"Oh, come on," Sam said, "that's a lot of crap. Once they're gone from this school, they're gone."

"No, no." Rawlins looked imploringly at Sam. "They told me that if I tell, then they got nothing to lose and they'll keep watching until I'm alone somewhere and then they'll tear me apart. They mean it, they really do. What am I going to do, Sam?"

"You've got to turn them in," Sam said. "They won't do anything to you once you tell, because that'll get them into a whole lot worse trouble than being expelled. If they tried anything like that, everybody would know who it was."

"No," Rawlins said, shaking his head. "I can't take the chance, you don't know how mean they are. Look." Tim lifted his shirt and then his undershirt and Sam saw an ugly red line going across Rawlins' stomach.

"A nail file," Tim said, hurriedly tucking in his clothes. "It hurt like hell."

"You can't just let this go on."

"That's why I told *you*," Rawlins said. "You're the one kid here who's not afraid of anything. Think of something, Sam, because I can't."

"I tell you." Sam was getting very annoyed. "All we have to do is go to my father."

"You promised!" Rawlins looked like he was going to cry. "You promised you wouldn't tell anybody."

"Oh, Jesus," Sam said.

Sitting in study hall two hours later, Sam felt cold disapproval aimed at him. Taking his own time to turn his head, Sam was not surprised to see that the chill came directly from the bleak green eyes of Mr. Kozodoy.

"Was that last night's dinner?" Mr. Kozodoy pointed a finger at the left-hand page of the social studies book in front of Sam. "Or perhaps it was this morning's breakfast?"

Sam hadn't paid any attention until then to the brown food stains on the page. There was also, as he looked closer, a tiny yellow lump of something in the crease of the book. He would have picked it up to smell it out of curiosity, but this didn't seem to be the time to do that.

"How do you think another student opening that book to that page will feel seeing all that gook on it?" Mr. Kozodoy sniffed in disgust.

"It's my book," Sam said. "The kids next year will get new books."

"Your answer is, first of all, insolent. And second, it is not to the point."

"It seems right on the point to me," Sam said, meeting Mr. Kozodoy's eyes.

"You are being insolent again," Mr. Kozodoy said. "You take books out of the library, don't you?"

"Sure, for reports and things."

"If I were to go through the shelves of this library and find all the books with nauseating remnants of food in their pages, whose name do you think would be most likely to appear on most of the cards listing the borrowers of those books?"

Sam was getting angry. "Jees, I'm not the only kid who has a snack sometimes when he's doing his homework."

"I am aware of that unhappy fact," Mr. Kozodoy said. "But in my experience of seven years here as a teacher, I have yet to come across any student who treats books as badly as you do. Look at this." He picked up Sam's social studies text. "*This* page is ripped. *These* pages look as if a small, vicious animal had chewed on them. *This* page is so full of ink spots that it is unreadable. And here," Mr. Kozodoy said, pulling out a tiny brown piece of apple, "is more of the food you insist on hoarding in your schoolbooks. Are you saving up for a famine? When all the rest of us are desperate with starvation, will you share your toothsome pages with us?"

"O.K., Mr. Kozodoy," Sam said, "I'll watch it. But, you know—"

"What do I know?"

"There's something friendly about a book that people have used while they're doing things they like to do. I mean, when I get a book out of the library and I come to a page with crumbs on it or Coke stains, I figure some kid before me had a good time while he was reading it. It's sort of like a message."

Mr. Kozodoy looked as if he were smelling something very unpleasant. "A message from one pack rat to another. Listen to me very carefully, young man. I am telling you this for your own good. He who is a slob in his personal habits is also a slob in his thinking habits. And he who is a slob in his thinking habits is a slob in his moral habits. It is all tied together. A clean boy is an honest boy. And vice versa."

"But that's silly." Sam could hardly believe what he was hearing. "That makes no sense. I know a boy who cheats all the time and he takes a bath every single day."

"A boy who is disrespectful of books," Mr. Kozodoy said, beginning to move away, "is disrespectful of learning, and a boy who is disrespectful of learning is disrespectful of teachers—as you again have just demonstrated."

Miss Sullivan walked into the teachers' lounge an hour later, went straight to the coffee machine, and poured herself a cup.

"This is one of those days," she announced to Mr. Kozodoy, who was looking through the *Times*. "I wish I had a long, thick, hard ruler. Like the nuns had to crack our heads with when I was going to school. I know, I know, 'The teacher who hits a child shows that she has a lot to learn about teaching.' There are other ways to enforce discipline, and all that. But I tell you, the teacher who hits a child feels a whole lot better than I do right now. Oh, that Sam!"

"The one and only Sam, the headmaster's son?" Miss Saperstein had joined Miss Sullivan at the coffee machine.

"The very one. Between the fights he gets into and his jumping up and down when he feels stupid because he doesn't understand the work and won't admit it, Sam is going to drive me out of my mind."

Mr. Kozodoy looked up from his paper. "Why do you put up with it? The headmaster has made it very clear that his ragamuffin son is to be treated just like every other boy here. Any time he disrupts your classroom, send him out! Let his father deal with him. There's no reason you should let him send you up the wall. You're not paid to teach chimpanzees."

"You don't understand," Miss Sullivan said as she poured herself more coffee. "I like that little nut. He's not a mean kid, which is more than I can say for some of the kids we have who are so well behaved in class. They don't cause *us* any trouble, but they can be awfully malicious with the other kids outside of class. Sam's not at all like that. But what does drive me up the wall about Sam is how hard it is to get him to concentrate just part of that enormous energy on his work."

"That is a rotten kid, period," Mr. Kozodoy said. "A self-indulgent, spoiled boy who always has to be the center of attention, who cannot—who will not—control his impulses, who is altogether insufferable. The headmaster may know how to deal with other people's children, though I have some doubts about that, but he certainly has let his own son grow wild.

"I suppose it's like psychiatrists' kids," Mr. Kozodoy continued. "Some of those need a psychiatrist to fix up what the psychiatrist at home didn't even begin to see was wrong with them. Come to think of it, I had another headmaster's son at Andover. He had been rushed to us from another school, and I could see why. When I had him in one of my classes, I felt like going in with a whip and a chair. After a while, I just threw him out of my class. Out! I refused to have anything more to do with that boy as long as I was at that school."

"Sam isn't anything like that," Miss Saperstein

shook her head. "Sure, he gets wild sometimes, but basically he's a good kid. My God, the other day he turned in some homework that was a revelation. That awful scrawl of his, and the way his papers usually look as if he'd just retrieved them from the garbage can where he'd left them overnight by mistake—all that had blinded me in the past to what the boy is capable of. I mean, he really had done an *A* paper.

"Of course, his work was as bad as ever the next day, because, he said, he hadn't had enough time to do it right because he had so many other assignments to do. The day before, through some fluke, mine was the only heavy homework he had."

"Nonsense!" Mr. Kozodoy said. "Someone else did that *A* paper for him."

"No," Miss Saperstein persisted, "it was Sam's work all right. I questioned him about it and he understood it all. And you know, when I told Sam what a first-class job he had done—the handwriting and spelling aside—he actually glowed. He *wants* to be a good boy, but so many other things get in the way and he's so easily distracted that most of the time he's all mixed up."

"That's right," Miss Sullivan said. "He never means to be bad. *That* I could deal with."

"Both of you are being soft-headed and sentimental about that miserable boy," Mr. Kozodoy said vehemently. "He's fresh, and he's tricky."

"Oh, no." Miss Sullivan shook her head in disagreement so hard that her glasses almost fell off. "One thing about Sam is that he's straightforward. Sometimes too straightforward."

"You watch," Mr. Kozodoy said. "You just watch. That boy is capable of anything."

5

"There were fourteen baseball cards, *including* Ted Williams." Fat Jake, standing with his back to Miss Sullivan's desk, glowered directly at Sam. "*Also* missing are two one-dollar bills and a Snoopy eraser, for God's sake!"

History class the following morning had begun with an announcement by Fat Jake that someone had gone through his desk.

"What else, Jake? What else that you don't want to tell us about?" a boy in the back shouted. Everyone laughed except Jake and Miss Sullivan.

"All of you think this is so damn funny," Jake shouted, obviously on the line between fury and tears. "Well, it's a hell of a thing when somebody in your own homeroom is a thief."

"We don't know that somebody here did it, Jake."

Miss Sullivan was opening her right-hand bottom drawer, where she had put the morning's bookclub money. "Who knows who might have come in during lunch period? Oh, my God!" She pulled the drawer all the way out. "The book money, it's gone! The order blanks with everyone's choices are here, but the money has disappeared."

"See," said Jake, triumphant. "We all got robbed."

Nobody was laughing anymore. "Well, I never—" Miss Sullivan shook her head.

"Search!" Jake bellowed. "Search! Everybody's got to be searched."

"I think that is probably a good idea," Miss Sullivan said. "Although I'm not entirely sure I have the authority..."

"We'll all volunteer," Jake was hopping up and down in his excitement. "Nobody who isn't a thief will mind being searched."

"How will we know which are Jake's dollar bills?" Sam asked. "You got the numbers of those dollar bills, Jake?"

"Fun-ny," Jake said as he looked toward Miss Sullivan, anxious for her to get the search underway.

She was shaking her head again. "No, I don't feel right searching children."

"Then I'm gonna call the cops," Jake announced.

"Come," Miss Sullivan said, motioning to Jake with her finger. "We'll go to the headmaster. He'll know what to do."

"What are you leaving us in your desk, Jake?" said a voice from the back rows.

Jake rushed back to his seat, opened his desk, took out a chocolate milk, two brownies, four comic books, and a large piece of rather moldy yellow cheese. He cradled it all in his arms as a number of the boys hooted. Someone solemnly recited the school rule about absolutely no food being allowed in a classroom under any circumstances except for birthday parties in the lower school.

"We shall have to have a talk about your desk," Miss Sullivan said to Jake as they reached the door.

"I lost a peach and a banana last spring," someone shouted. "Search that boy on the way to the headmaster's!"

Jake turned around and would have shaken his fist if his hands hadn't been so full.

"Have you any idea what's going on?" the headmaster asked Sam that night as he passed the frankfurters and beans.

"You mean the stealing in our room today?" Sam said.

"Yes, I mean the stealing, and not only in your room. A girl in one of the fifth-grade classes had a ten-dollar bill when she came to school this morning, and some thief has it now. You know I don't ask you questions about ordinary things that go wrong. I don't expect my son to be my eyes and ears in the school. It's *my* responsibility to know what's going on. But stealing is not an ordinary thing, and the suspicion it creates and feeds on is poisonous—in a school or anywhere else."

"Uh-huh," said Sam, who was losing his appetite.

"In your own ornery way, Sam," the headmaster said, "you have pride in Alcott, no matter how much you say you hate the school. So I am asking you as an Alcott boy—and that means an honest boy—to tell me anything you know."

Sam sighed. "If I knew anything, I'd tell you, dad, but I don't."

The headmaster kept looking at his son until Sam lowered his eyes. "You haven't the slightest clue?" he persisted.

"No, I really don't," Sam said. "Maybe though"—he reddened slightly—"somebody is making some kids steal things."

"What do you mean by that?" the headmaster asked sharply.

"Nothing. I hear about that sort of thing in other schools once in a while, and I just thought maybe something like that might be going on at Alcott."

"Just like that, the idea came to you, huh?" His father was still staring at him.

Sam thought hard about the terror in Rawlins' eyes when he made Sam promise not to say anything about what Brompton, Howes, and Maguire were doing. If Rawlins could have stolen from his own father, he could have swiped something from a kid's desk. Damn it, Sam sighed again, he knew he shouldn't have made that promise. Still, he had no proof Rawlins was the thief. It *could* have been somebody else. Any way you look at it, Sam thought as he pushed his plate away, that promise had to be kept.

"There's something you know about this that I ought to know." The headmaster spoke very distinctly and very softly.

Sam wished he'd yell. It's a lot easier not to tell somebody what he wants to know when he's yelling at you.

Sam's mother had been looking back and forth between her husband and her son. "I do wish you'd put Sam in another school," she said. "Other boys have a rest from the headmaster when they come home."

Yea, mom! Sam cheered silently.

"Sam can take it," the headmaster said. "He's a tough boy, right, Sam?"

"I wish you'd lay off," Sam said. "I don't know anything about it."

"I think you do." The headmaster tried to catch Sam's eye again. "I think you were telling me you know something when you said someone might be forcing kids to steal. I think there's a shakedown going on at Alcott."

"What do you mean, 'shakedown'?" Sam was using every bit of strength he had to keep from showing the panic growing in him.

"You know what I mean," the headmaster said, beginning to raise his voice. "Bullies ganging up on a kid to make him give them money."

"No." Sam's mouth felt very dry. "No, I haven't seen anything like that."

"I'll give you something to think about." Sam's father leaned across the table and poked a finger into his son's chest. "If there is something like that going on at Alcott, the probability is that more than one victim is involved. Bullies swell up on other people's fear. So if you know something that you're not telling me, you are helping those bullies victimize God knows how many kids. By your silence, you are an accomplice. I want you to keep that in mind. I want the weight of your responsibility to grow heavier and heavier in your mind until you can't think of anything else."

"Carl," Sam's mother broke in. "That's your son you're doing this to."

"If I'm correct in my assumptions," the headmaster said, "Sam is doing this to himself. A decent boy does not remain silent, for whatever reason, when the safety of others is involved."

Sam loved frankfurters and beans, but he hadn't had a bite. At that moment, even ice cream would have made him want to throw up.

"Can I be excused?" Sam asked.

"No," the headmaster answered. "You know how I feel about good food going to waste."

Sam looked desperately at his mother.

"Please, Carl," Liz Davidson said. "Nothing is going to be gained by making the boy get sick."

"Why should he get sick," the headmaster drummed his fingers on the table, "if he hasn't done anything he finds hard to hold down? And why are you perspiring, dear boy?"

"Damn it," Sam stood up, "I don't know *anything*. Can't you understand that?"

"One. There will be no swearing at this table," the headmaster began. "Two. You will eat everything on that plate."

"If I eat anything on that plate," Sam said, "I will throw up on your plate and all over the table."

The headmaster pulled in his cheeks to keep from smiling. "All right, you may be excused," he said. "But remember, if there is a shakedown gang, *you,* so long as you remain silent, are one of them."

6

Around twelve thirty the next day Benjy and Blake, not having seen Sam in the lunchroom, went looking for him. As they prowled the corridors, Benjy said he'd heard that some desks in a fourth-grade room had been rifled that morning while the kids were on a class trip.

"I bet I'm suspect number one," Blake said, looking sidelong at Benjy.

"The hell you are," Benjy said. "This school would rather have the building stolen piece by piece than admit that a scholarship student, for crissake, could be so ungrateful that he'd go through the kids' desks."

"Now, then," Blake stopped, "how do you know that I don't know that, and so-o-o, having a perfect cover, I am indeed the mysterious master criminal?"

"Because you're not a sneak, that's why," Benjy said. "You've got a big mouth, like Sam. You're not as tough as you think you are. You're full of it in other ways, but whatever you do, you don't hide it. You act like everything you do ought to be on TV."

Blake laughed. "Well, the thing is, I am too damn smart to get my ass busted for a couple of dollars. Whoever is doing this has got to be plain dumb. And that leaves you with a whole lot of candidates in this school."

Finally, Blake and Benjy found Sam downstairs, standing outside the school door.

"Where you fellows going?" the guard asked as they passed his desk near the entrance. "You know the rules: nobody but seniors can leave during the day, and they got to have passes."

"Give a guy a uniform," Blake muttered to Benjy, "and he acts like he was born wearing it." Turning to the guard, Blake said, "We're not going anywhere. We just want some air."

"I'll be watching you," the guard said suspiciously.

"You do that," Blake answered. "I ain't got my mama to watch me when I'm down here, so you be my mama."

"Now watch it, boy," the guard said, bristling.

"I thought all you folks were brothers," Benjy said to Blake.

"Shows how little you know, Benjy," Blake answered.

"Where were you?" Blake asked Sam, who was leaning against the wall, staring at the traffic.

"Wasn't hungry," Sam said. "Listen, you guys, I want some advice. Suppose somebody you know comes up to you and says he's got a big problem, but he won't tell you about it unless you swear you won't tell anybody else."

"That's dumb," Blake said. "I don't agree to nothing until I know every bit of what I'm agreeing to. I don't go into things blind."

"O.K.," Sam said peevishly, "suppose you *had* been dumb and you went along with it."

"Uh-huh," Blake looked at Sam. "Let's suppose instead that *you* were dumb and *you* went along with it. Why don't you tell the story that way."

"Forget it," Sam said in disgust.

"No, come on," Benjy urged. "Go ahead."

"Well," Sam said, "so you swear you're not going to say a word and you find out this kid is being forced by some bigger kids to do something wrong, real wrong. But you've promised you won't tell."

"Once you give your word, dumb as you are to give your word before you know what's coming down," Blake said, "you are stuck."

"Unless," Benjy said thoughtfully, "keeping quiet gets you yourself into trouble."

"Even then," Blake insisted, "once you give your word, you give the main thing you got. No matter what."

"I understand that," Benjy said, "but there are exceptions to everything."

"Sure," Blake smiled, "you can exception yourself out of anything, but man, a guy gives me his promise and he breaks it, he's dead, far as I'm concerned. I don't want nothing to do with him ever again. He can yell 'exception' until he can't yell no more, but I know what he is—he's a fink."

"You guys sure are a lot of help," Sam said impatiently and went back into the building. He walked slowly to his next class. On the landing between the second and third floors, he saw Tim Rawlins moving quickly up the stairs.

"They still after you?" Sam asked as he drew alongside Rawlins.

Rawlins nodded and looked pleadingly at Sam. "Have you thought of anything yet?" he asked.

"No," Sam said. "I still think the only thing to do is to report them."

"No," Rawlins answered in a squeaky voice, "I can't take the chance."

"Do you know if those bastards are doing this to anyone else?" Sam asked.

"They say they are," Rawlins answered. "They say I'm the slowest payer of all the kids they've got."

"How many kids are they shaking down?"

"I don't know," Rawlins said. "But I don't think they're making it up when they say there's more than me."

"I don't either," Sam scratched his head. "Say, where are you getting the money now to pay those bloodsuckers?"

"I'm way behind," Rawlins said. "And I'm scared, Sam. Really scared."

Coming toward them was Fred Brompton's huge older brother, Marty, whose crushing tackles the Saturday before had had a great deal to do with Alcott being able to stay unbeaten this season.

"Jees," Sam said to Rawlins, "if they ever want to make another King Kong movie, there's the star. Except for that pig face." Sam pretended to be looking at Marty through a viewfinder. "Yeah, he's got to wear a mask."

Rawlins half smiled as Sam chuckled at his own lines.

"What's so funny?" Brompton said, stopping in front of Sam.

"Nothing," Sam said. "I was just trying to figure out if one camera could fit all of you into one shot. I think it would take at least two cameras though."

"Not funny. Not funny at all." Marty shot a big hand out and made a sharp downward motion in front of Sam. "There," he said, "the camera's broken. Understand?"

"I always have more." Sam pantomimed taking a camera bag off his shoulder, reaching into it, and taking out another camera.

"If you weren't so little, punk, I'd push your nose into the back of your head—for real." Marty Brompton moved his bulk closer, but Sam stood his ground. "One day, punk, you'll get it. You'll get it good." Brompton cuffed Sam's ear and walked on.

"I never did get my baseball cards back, you know," Jake said to Sam an hour later as they came off the basketball court.

Sam stopped short and shoved his elbow into Jake's considerable stomach. "Are you calling me a thief?" he yelled in Jake's ear.

"Break it up, break it up." Mr. Rogolow hurried over. This year he was more or less celebrating his twentieth year as Alcott's gym teacher. "I saw it, Sam. I saw that elbow. You're just as quick with that elbow as you are with your little fists. How many times have I told you guys not to roughhouse in here?"

"This makes," Sam said, shutting his eyes in intense concentration, "three hundred and twelve times."

"You are some wise guy," Mr. Rogolow said. "I want an apology for that."

"You got no sense of humor?" Sam was bouncing on the balls of his feet.

"Now look, you jack-in-the-box," Mr. Rogolow said, towering over Sam, "nobody gets away with disrespecting me." Sam kept bouncing.

"My pants! My pants!" Jake was standing in front of his locker, shouting. "And my shirt! And my socks! And my sho-o-o-es!" His locker was empty.

"O.K.," Mr. Rogolow said. He put his hands on his hips. "Everybody open his locker door. *Now*!"

"Have you got a right to look in our lockers?" Benjy asked.

"Yeah," Blake said, winking at Benjy. "Where's your search warrant, Mr. Rogolow? We know our rights."

"Search the lockers! Search the lockers!" Jake yelled. "Every single one of them."

"That kid is really queer for searching," Benjy said.

"A real search freak," Sam added.

Mr. Rogolow was breathing hard. "I bet you know all about search warrants," he snapped at Blake. "Oh, Jesus." Mr. Rogolow looked sick as Blake's blackness became all he could see in the room. "I'm sorry. I apologize. I really do."

"Not accepted," Blake said, turning his back on the gym teacher and walking toward his locker. "And you do *not* have my permission to search my locker."

"Mine either," said Sam, running to his locker and

standing in front of it with his hands, like Blake's, folded across his chest.

"You." Mr. Rogolow turned to Sam. "Butt out of this."

"Nobody's locker has to be searched," announced Benjy, as he came out of the bathroom grinning. "The search freak's clothes are in there."

"What's in where?" Jake yowled, rushing into the bathroom. "O my God, they're in the toilet. All my clothes are in the toilet."

"Now that's a hell of a thing to do to a schoolmate," Mr. Rogolow said, shaking his head in disgust. "Anybody here man enough to own up to that rotten, cowardly act?"

"We're all just boys," Sam said, "and like you're always telling us, there are days when you can hardly tell a boy from an orangutan."

"I still want to look into your locker." Mr. Rogolow advanced on Sam.

"No way," Sam tightened his hands across his chest. Blake moved over beside him, as did Benjy.

"So that's the way it is?" Mr. Rogolow glared at them. "We'll just see what the headmaster says about this. There's something mighty suspicious about a boy who won't let his locker be searched."

"Then that applies to me too." Blake glared back at him.

"I already apologized to you," Mr. Rogolow said impatiently. "You're not part of this."

"That's no news," Blake said.

"Touchy, touchy." Mr. Rogolow made clicking noises with his tongue. "You people are so touchy."

Blake spat at him.

"Whoa now, whoa now." Mr. Rogolow's face looked like a tomato coming apart. "In all my years in this school, nobody has ever—"

"Who you telling to whoa? I'm no horse," Blake said icily.

"Are you going to search that rotten Sam's locker or are you not going to search that rotten Sam's locker? I bet you my fourteen baseball cards and my two one-dollar bills are in there!" Jake, his sopping wet clothes at his feet, howled at Mr. Rogolow while shaking his fist at everybody else.

"Sam has already told us he will not permit his locker to be searched," Mr. Rogolow said. "And we will remember that."

"It's a matter of principle," Sam said.

"Sure," Mr. Rogolow said nastily, "the principle of not getting caught."

"Yow!" Jake, looking at the floor behind him, was roaring. "Somebody stole my clothes again!"

"I just want you to know," Mr. Rogolow said, sounding very aggrieved, "that in all my years here, you are the most obnoxious boys I have ever seen."

"Thank you, sir," Sam said, standing fast in front of his locker.

7

Later that day, Sam was in the library brooding rather than reading. He looked out the window and saw that across the street Fred Brompton, George Howes, and Bill Maguire were crowding around an obviously frightened younger boy who was not Tim Rawlins. Quickly shoving his math assignment and his loose-leaf notebook into his book bag, Sam ran out of the library and careened into Mr. Kozodoy in the hall. The teacher fell back against the wall. As he regained his balance, Mr. Kozodoy startled himself by aiming a kick at Sam, who by then was well out of reach.

Down the stairs, past the open-mouthed school guard, Sam landed on the sidewalk. Brompton, Howes, and Maguire, laughing now, were still across the street, leaning against a building. Their victim, however, had disappeared.

All Sam had had in his mind was that the boy needed help and that his tormentors wouldn't keep on hassling him in front of a witness. Now, frustrated, heart pounding, Sam felt something pushing him to confront the three tenth-graders anyway. What the hell, Sam reassured himself as he crossed the street, they're not going to get rough with the headmaster's son. Hey, he thought suddenly, that's not *always* a bad position to be in. He walked faster.

"Something you wanted?" said Bill Maguire, tall, muscular, his face full of acne.

"Yeah, to what do we owe this honor?" Short, wiry, his face fixed in a most unpleasant smile, George Howes stepped in front of Sam. Fred Brompton, big and broad, like a football with a head and feet glued on, slouched against the wall, eyes half closed, silent.

"What were you doing with that kid?" Sam tried to make his voice deeper, but it cracked halfway through the sentence.

"What kid?" Frowning, Maguire looked at Howes. "You see any kid around here?"

"Just crazy young Davidson, right there." Howes put a finger on the tip of Sam's nose and pressed down hard until Sam shook it away.

"Think harder," Brompton rumbled. "We mustn't be impolite to crazy young Davidson, considering who he is."

"Oh, he's a regular guy," Maguire put a hand on Sam's shoulder. Sam shook that off too. "But today," Maguire tried to look sad, "he's unfriendly for some reason. That hurts my feelings. Doesn't that hurt your feelings?" Maguire looked at Brompton.

"What did you think we were doing to that kid who wasn't here?" Brompton moved away from the wall and pressed against Sam, who stumbled back.

"Shaking him down for money, like—" Sam stopped, but not soon enough.

"Go on, crazy Davidson." Maguire's face was stiff except for his eyes, which kept moving from Sam to Howes and Brompton and back again to Sam. "Go *on,*" he barked.

"So that's why you're so down on us," Howes said. "Now where did you get that nutty idea?"

"Yeah, what a terrible thing to say about three of your fellow Alcott boys." Brompton looked down at Sam. "But you said it. Now you've got to tell us why."

"I don't have to tell you guys anything." Sam began to move farther back.

"Who else have you told that stupid lie to?" Brompton came after Sam.

"Nobody," Sam said, remembering Tim Rawlins' fear. "And that's the truth."

"I sure hope it's the truth," Brompton kept staring at Sam. "Unless, of course, you think you've got some kind of proof. You can't just accuse us of something that could get us thrown out of school without telling us why you're spreading such goddamn lies."

"I told you," Sam said, "I'm not spreading anything."

"Hold it," Maguire said loftily, motioning to Brompton and Howes. "I think I know what happened. Somebody told Davidson this wild story, and he believed it." Maguire looked at Sam. "So all we want to know is who started this whole stupid lie. I mean, you can't just spring something like that on us and walk away."

"The hell I can't!" Sam shouted as he leaped into the street, where he nearly got hit by a bus. He ran full-speed into the school.

"Hold on," the school guard stepped in front of him. "I got to mark you down, Sam. Unless you got a pass to show me."

"What about those three guys across the street?" Sam was jumping up and down. "What about *them*? They show you a pass?"

"What three guys across the street?" the guard looked out the door. Brompton, Howes, and Maguire had disappeared.

"Oh, shit!" Sam said, throwing his book bag on the floor.

"I got to mark you down again, Sam." The guard took a pen out of his shirt pocket. "You know the rule about using bad language on school property. And you, the headmaster's son!"

Dragging his book bag behind him, Sam began moving slowly up the stairs until he saw the clock on the wall of the second-floor corridor.

Damn, Sam thought. I'm late—and for Kozodoy! Terrific.

Sam crept in the back door of the classroom. But as he feared and expected, Mr. Kozodoy stopped in mid-sentence as soon as he saw Sam.

"Undoubtedly you were detained by a message from the mayor," Mr. Kozodoy said caustically. "I read this morning in the *Times* that the mayor is a dinner guest this evening at the White House. He must have called for your advice on what to wear."

Fat Jake snickered. Blake pantomimed uproarious laughter, his mouth opening in huge, silent guffaws as he clutched at his stomach. The rest of the class tensed in anticipation, waiting to hear Sam's response and waiting to see how soon he'd be gunned down. Before he bit the dust, Sam was always good for a few laughs.

Not today though. "I'm sorry," Sam said to Mr. Kozodoy, "I forgot what time it was."

"You don't have a watch?" Mr. Kozodoy asked solicitously.

"I lost it," Sam said. "I'm always losing them."

"Them! Them!" Mr. Kozodoy sounded like a clock that marked the hours with a thud rather than a gong. "How fortunate you are to have parents who keep making up for your carelessness."

"I only lost two watches. Then they said I couldn't have another one for a year."

"*Poor* child," Mr. Kozodoy said, to the obbligato of Fat Jake's giggling. "Why are you tardy?" Mr. Kozodoy suddenly shouted.

"I told you," Sam said, sitting down. "I was thinking of something else and I just plain forgot."

"I did not say you could sit down!" Mr. Kozodoy boomed. "I have not yet decided whether you are to remain in this class after showing your contempt of us by slithering in late. Get *up*, young man!"

Sam rose slowly. His head aimed at Mr. Kozodoy, his lower lip thrust out, Sam half shouted, "What do you mean *contempt*? I said I was sorry, and I didn't *slither*."

"Boys who come in the back door after the class is already in session," Mr. Kozodoy said firmly, "are known as slithering boys. It is a well-known term in the history of pedagogy. Sit down, *slitherer!*"

For a moment Sam seemed suspended in mid-air, torn between obeying and storming out of the room. With a strange sound, something between a moan and a growl, he sank into his seat.

"As I was saying," Mr. Kozodoy went on, addressing the rest of the class as he walked back and forth in front of his desk, "the First Amendment to the Constitution guarantees every citizen of this republic the right to free speech. Now, there are those who interpret the First Amendment as meaning that freedom of speech is absolute, that no one can *ever* be punished for *anything* he says—so long as he just says it. He can *call* for violence. He can get up on a platform and *urge* people to do terrible things, unlawful things, but as long as he is just talking—as long as he himself does not *do* any of the awful things he is asking others to do—he is free to keep on talking without the slightest penalty.

"However," Mr. Kozodoy continued, quickening his pace, "for much of this century, the majority of the Supreme Court has held that there are limits to free speech *if* the exercise of speech constitutes a *clear and present danger* to others. For example, as Justice Oliver Wendell Holmes said in 1919, writing a unanimous opinion for the Court in a case known as *Schenck versus United States,* 'The most stringent protection of free speech would not protect a man in falsely shouting fire in a theater and causing a panic.'

"Now think about that illustration," Mr. Kozodoy

said as he leaned forward. "Think carefully. If a man falsely shouts fire in a theater, the *danger* is present and it is *clear*. He is not alone in the theater. There is a crowd in that theater and if he yells fire falsely, thereby causing a panic, some people will very likely be injured, maybe even trampled to death. So, anyone so foolish, so irresponsible, as to cry fire falsely in such circumstances could indeed be punished. His exercise of speech, in that specific instance, is *not* protected by the First Amendment."

Fat Jake's hand shot up. But too impatient to wait to be acknowledged, he burst out, "Like Sam yelling in the lunchroom the other day that his dental appliance was somewhere in the macaroni!"

"Yes," Mr. Kozodoy beamed at Jake. "That is a foolish exercise of free speech and therefore is not protected."

"But that's not the same as yelling fire in a crowded theater," Benjy volunteered. "There wasn't any chance that anyone in the lunchroom would be hurt because of what Sam said."

"Of course there was!" Jake, in his enthusiasm, stood up to make his point more forcefully. "There could have been a panic with everybody trying to get out of there at once before they threw up."

Everyone laughed, including Sam.

"I will grant you, Benjy," Mr. Kozodoy said, "that the analogy between a false cry of fire, on the one hand, and the false cry of a dental appliance being lost in the macaroni, on the other hand, is not exact. I bespoke myself too soon. If Sam had committed that dumb joke in a public place, he probably could not have been punished because it might be difficult to prove that his foolishness constituted a clear and present danger to others, other than an abrupt loss of appetite. But Alcott is a *private* school and so he was properly punished by Mr. McEvoy who placed him on detention. A quite light punishment, in my opinion."

Benjy, suddenly struck with new, unwelcome knowledge, asked, "Do you mean that by going to a private school, we give up our First Amendment rights?"

"I differ with the Supreme Court," Mr. Kozodoy answered. "I do not believe children *ever* have any constitutional rights. Children are too immature to be considered full citizens. But in recent years, the Supreme Court seems to be saying that children in public schools do have certain constitutional rights. But not in private schools, thank God. So the answer to your question, Benjy, is yes. By going to a private school, you have only those First Amendment rights that we, the teachers and the headmaster, grant you."

"You mean private schools are dictatorships?" Sam said accusingly.

"A characteristically crude and inaccurate way of putting it, young man," Mr. Kozodoy said curtly. "No, Alcott is not a dictatorship. But we teachers and administrators do function in this school *in loco parentis*. That is, we act toward you, during the time you are in the school, in place of your parents. We decide, as they do at home, which rights and privileges you are to have—and which rights and privileges you lose if you misbehave. And for how long you lose them. And we decide what other punishments you deserve if you misbehave.

"None of you, I hope, has absolute free speech at home. There are some words you cannot say in front of your parents without being punished for that abuse of speech. At least, that's the way it used to be in good homes. Similarly, there are some words you cannot say in this school without being punished."

"I think I know what you're saying," said a boy in the first row. "But I'm still kind of confused. In assembly last week, the headmaster told us that the most important purpose of education is to get us prepared to be free citizens in a democracy. But you're saying that you and the other teachers and the headmaster can take away any of our rights, just like our parents can. So where are we going to learn how to be free citizens? In the street?"

Sam, Blake, and Benjy applauded.

Mr. Kozodoy first frowned at the applauders. Then with a slight smile, he said, "There are some experiences that are too important to be exposed too soon to full democratic processes. An education that is intended to transform raw boys into free, mature citizens is one of those experiences."

Fat Jake squinted in his puzzlement. "You mean we learn to be free by first not being free."

"Let me put it this way," Mr. Kozodoy said. "When you plant a crop, you sow your seeds in neat rows. You then cultivate them. You tend them. You control them. You don't just throw the seeds any which way, and then just let them grow any which way."

"You're talking about two different things," Sam said loudly from the back of the room. "Seeds don't think. Seeds don't have things to say. Seeds are just *there* to grow into something that's going to be eaten.

Seeds aren't the same as human beings. What you're saying doesn't make sense."

"Oh, it wouldn't make sense to *you*," Mr. Kozodoy answered, savoring his words, "since you so obviously do not have enough sense yet to be a citizen. *You* are going to need a lot of cultivation, a lot of tending, if you're ever going to make it."

"Fire! Fire!" Sam shouted.

Only a few kids laughed.

"Thank you, young man," Mr. Kozodoy said coldly. "You have just proved my point once more."

8

Brooding, Sam came out of Mr. Kozodoy's class and ran into Blake.

"They caught the damn fool thief," Blake whispered.

"Who? Who is he?" Sam, sure he knew the name, felt a chill.

"Rawlins. Tim Rawlins," Blake said. "I always figured there was something sneaky about him."

"Goddamn!" Sam shook his head.

"You knew something about it?" Blake cocked his head and looked at Sam curiously.

"Just tell me what happened."

"Well, I heard somebody crying and carrying on," Blake said. "Then I saw Kozodoy with his hand, like it was a manacle, around that skinny dude's wrist. Kozodoy was pulling and hauling him down the corridor. To your father's office, I guess. This Rawlins dude was yelling, between bawling, 'They *made* me do it. They *made* me steal.' And every time he said that, Kozodoy would give him an extra yank and say, 'Who? Who made you do it?' And the poor little bastard would shake his head, refuse to tell and start bawling again.

"One of the kids watching with me said Kozodoy had been going past an empty homeroom and saw this Rawlins loser going through the desks. So that's all I know. Like I asked you before, do you know anything about it?"

"No." Sam turned his eyes away.

"The hell you don't," Blake said angrily. "You must think I'm some kind of fool, trying to con me like that."

"Aw, Blake," Sam said, squirming, "I can't tell you, O.K.? I just can't tell anyone."

"Now that's something else," Blake said with a grin. "I just don't like to be taken for a fool. Well, whatever you two got between you, your skinny friend is in one hell of a lot of trouble."

"Yeah," said Sam, looking at the ground, and shaking his head again.

"And I'll tell you something else," Blake continued, "he's not the only thief around here."

"What do you mean?"

"I was walking past an empty room yesterday and I saw another little dude, littler even than Rawlins, whipping through the desks like he'd had a lot of practice. You know the dude I mean. That fourth-grader who always has that big, black briefcase and talks like a dictionary."

"Yeah," said Sam, "I've seen that kid. Never would have figured *him* for a thief, though. Anyway, you mean to tell me you just let him go ahead and do it?" Sam's voice had become a squeak.

"Soon as the little fellow saw me," Blake said, "he scooted out of there, briefcase and all. Hell, I wasn't about to turn him in. If it had been *my* homeroom and *my* desk he was going through, he'd have walked out of there sideways and very slow after I'd gotten through with him. I take care of my business and I don't mess with anybody else's unless they mess with me. You got some objection?"

"No," Sam said, "I'm no hero in this either."

A few doors away from where Sam and Blake were walking in the corridor, Tim Rawlins stood in front of the headmaster's desk. His hands were clenched, his heart was pounding.

"Let's go over it again," the headmaster said. "You told Mr. Kozodoy that 'they' made you do it. 'They' made you steal. 'They' have names. What are their names?"

Rawlins kept his lips pressed tightly together and stared at the wall over the headmaster's head.

"*Why* did these mysterious 'they' make you steal?" the headmaster asked.

"That's not quite right," Rawlins' voice trembled. "They didn't tell me to steal. They told me I had to give them money. And the only way I could get that money was to steal."

"Why do you keep refusing to tell me who 'they' are?" the headmaster persisted.

"Because," Rawlins took a deep, sighing breath, "they would break me in two if I told who they are. That's what they said they'd do, and they would do it, sir."

"No, they—whoever they are—would *not* do it, Rawlins," the headmaster said impatiently. "I would see to that. I guarantee you no harm will come to you."

"I don't mean to sound disrespectful, sir"—Rawlins' voice could barely be heard—"but you don't know them. You couldn't protect me *everywhere* I went. Nobody could. Sooner or later, they'd get me."

"What do you mean, I don't know them?" the headmaster was visibly irritated. "All I don't know is their names. They're Alcott boys, so I do know them, once I find out their goddamn names. Anyway, whoever they are, I will make certain there are no reprisals against you. And I will assure those hooligans, because I am going to find out who they are, that if they so much as threaten an Alcott boy from this point on, I shall bring criminal charges against them. Once more, Rawlins, their names! I intend to have their names."

Rawlins, now staring at the clock, following the inexorable second hand, said nothing.

"Mr. Rawlins," the headmaster spoke very clearly, "I want to be absolutely sure that you know exactly what your choices are. You have only two. You will either give me their names or you will be expelled from this school. Not suspended. Expelled. And there will be no way you can ever come back. And other schools will know that you have been expelled. I shall give you until eight thirty tomorrow morning, in this office, to make your decision."

Rawlins' shoulders slumped. He turned around and walked toward the door.

"One more thing," the headmaster said. "Did my son know anything about this?"

Rawlins froze. Then he began to shake.

"I see," the headmaster said, rubbing his forehead. "How much of this did Sam know about?"

Rawlins kept his back to the headmaster. In a hoarse whisper, he finally said, "N-n-nothing."

"That's something else you have until tomorrow at eight thirty to tell me the truth about." The headmaster got up from his chair, turned around, and looked out the window.

After leaving the headmaster's office, Tim Rawlins kept walking until he turned the corner. There he stopped, fell against the wall, steadied himself, put his hand over his eyes, breathed deeply, breathed deeply again, and let the tears come.

"Aw, look at that," Fred Brompton said softly, solemnly. "Something's bothering our boy Rawlins."

"Yeah," Maguire said, picking up Brompton's funereal tone. "Tell us all about it, Rawlins. We're your *friends*."

Howes, standing behind Brompton and Maguire, just grinned.

"We heard you got busted by Kozodoy." Brompton had become hard and businesslike. "And we heard you got taken to the headmaster. This isn't the place to talk about it. Now, you listen close." Brompton took Rawlins' jaw and pressed his fingers into the boy's face.

"Meet us at Max's tonight. At eight. Right on the nose. *Eight*."

Rawlins stared at Brompton, his fear so open, his look so hopeless, that Howes stopped grinning.

"You be there." Brompton had pulled Rawlins' face toward him and was now also squeezing the back of his neck, "Or else we will find you and we will beat the shit out of you. Understand?"

Rawlins nodded weakly and watched in despair as the three walked away.

"Are you sick?" Mrs. Davidson asked as her husband came in the door. "It's only five thirty. The last time you came home early on a school day, it turned out you had walking pneumonia, and you wound up in bed for a week. And you are a miserable patient. Let me take your temperature."

"There's nothing wrong with me," the headmaster said irritably. "Not physically, anyway. Where's Sam?"

"In his room, presumably doing his homework."

"Come on," her husband said, "I need you in this."

They paused at the door, to which was Scotch taped a large piece of yellow construction paper. Written boldly with a black felt pen were the instructions:

PLEASE KNOCK BEFORE ENTRING
THIS MEANS EVEREYBODY!
SAM
EVEREYBODY!

His father shook his head at the spelling and knocked.

"Who's there?" Sam asked.

As Mr. Davidson opened the door, Sam was in the process of switching off the radio which was perched on an unopened math book. Sam looked at his parents.

"You swore there'd be no radio until every bit of your homework was done!" Sam's mother said in loud annoyance.

"Never mind about that now," Mr. Davidson interrupted. "There's something much more important. Sam, you heard about Rawlins being caught this afternoon?"

"Caught at what?" his wife asked.

"Stealing," her husband answered brusquely. "Sam, I must have a completely truthful answer to this question. I *must* have it, do you understand? What do you know of Rawlins' involvement in the stealing that's been going on?"

Sam looked at his father, scratched his head, scratched his neck, bit his lip, and said, "I—I can't say."

"What the hell do you mean, you can't say?" His father strode to where Sam was sitting at his desk.

"You've already said *something*, Sam." His mother's voice was gentle. "Saying you can't say anything means you do know something but won't tell us."

"Precisely." Sam's father put his hand on the boy's shoulder. Sam flinched slightly. "Sam, I don't think I have to tell you how serious this is. Rawlins is in very, very deep trouble. And so is Alcott until I can find out everything there is to be found about the stealing. As I told you before, my strong suspicion is that some thugs—some Alcott thugs, I am dismayed to say— are shaking Rawlins down, and probably other boys as well. Sam, I have reason to believe you know something about it."

"What do you mean, 'reason to believe'?" Sam said, trying to look offended.

"I asked Rawlins if you knew anything about this—"

"And what did he say?" Sam broke in.

"He said you knew nothing, but the *way* in which he said it made it clear to me that you *do* have some information, at least about Rawlins. Sam, I must know."

Sam scratched his head hard, picked his nose, looked out the window, started to speak, stopped, and started again. "Rawlins was right," Sam said slowly. "I don't know nothing about it."

"I'd think that was a deliberate double negative," his father said, "if I thought you knew what a double negative is."

"Sam," Mrs. Davidson said as she stroked her son's hair, "Sam, you never tell lies. Oh, you try to once in a while, but you just can't pull it off. And I'm very proud of the fact that I can always believe what you say. I also know how you feel about breaking a promise. But Sam, telling a lie is worse than breaking a promise. Especially now, when it means so much to your father and to me and to young Rawlins, too. You've got to tell us the truth."

Sam turned his head away. "Rawlins said I don't know nothing about it," Sam said to the wall. "So I don't know nothing about it."

9

Tim Rawlins was feeling miserable enough without its being dark and cold too. That evening, huddling in the doorway of Max's, the closed candy store around the corner from the school, he looked at the lighted windows in an apartment house across the street. Rawlins envied the kids who were warm and safe inside.

He looked at his watch. They were late. Rawlins shivered in the cold. I wonder if they'd take my watch in place of the money I owe them. Owe them? I don't owe them anything, he thought bitterly. If I wasn't such a damn coward, I wouldn't be here. I'd be home having dinner and looking out the window, glad to be inside. Jesus, I forgot. What am I going to tell my parents when I finally do get home?

"This poor little boy is cold." Fred Brompton, followed by Howes and Maguire, moved into the doorway, pushing Rawlins into a corner.

"What did you tell the headmaster this afternoon?" Brompton jammed an elbow into Rawlins' side. "And don't lie. We want to know every word."

"I didn't tell him anything," said Rawlins. His teeth were clattering more from fear now than from the cold. "Nothing, nothing at all."

"And he just patted you on the head and gave you a lollipop, is that what he did?" Brompton elbowed him again.

"No," Rawlins closed his eyes and mumbled, "he said I have to tell him—"

"Louder!" Howes ordered.

"HE SAID I HAVE TO TELL HIM BY HALF PAST EIGHT TOMORROW WHO MADE ME DO IT OR ELSE—"

A woman, passing by, looked sharply at the four boys.

"Lower, keep your voice *lower*," Maguire whispered in Rawlins' ear. Brompton smiled ingratiatingly at the woman who smiled back as she went on her way.

"What makes the headmaster think somebody *made* you steal?" Maguire pushed his face into Rawlins'.

"I—I—I wasn't thinking," Rawlins answered. "I just said that when Mr. Kozodoy grabbed me, and he told the headmaster."

"You punk!" Brompton punched Rawlins hard in the stomach.

"What happens if you don't tell him?" Howes asked.

"I'll be expelled." Rawlins' voice was very low.

"Well, we can't have that, can we?" Brompton said. "We wouldn't want to lose you, Rawlins. We've become quite attached to you, haven't we? What are you going to tell the headmaster tomorrow?"

"I don't *know*," Rawlins wailed.

"*We* know," Brompton said. "You are going to tell the headmaster that this terrible bully, this disgrace to Alcott, this *monster* who made you steal is his crazy son, Sam."

"Sam!" Rawlins shouted in shock and protest.

Maguire clapped a hand over Rawlins' mouth, dug him in the ribs again, and whispered, "Keep your voice *down*, you little bastard. You're going to be talking real soft from now on, right?" Rawlins nodded in agreement, and Maguire removed his hand.

"I *can't* say it was Sam." Rawlins' voice was pleading. "I just can't. He's the only one—"

"You told about us," Brompton finished the sentence. "I *thought* it must have been you."

"He promised not to tell anybody, not even his father," Rawlins wailed.

"I bet he kept his promise," Maguire grinned. "He's a real straight arrow that one. You picked a real winner when you went to Sam for help."

"O.K., Rawlins," Brompton said. "It'll be your word against his, and the headmaster is going to have to bend over backward to be fair when it comes to deciding whether his own son is a thief. All clear, punk?" He stared at Rawlins.

"I won't! I won't!" Rawlins struggled to get out of the corner of the doorway into which he had been pressed. But the massed bulk of the three older boys would not budge.

"You *will*," Brompton said decisively. "You will.

Because otherwise, we will break every one of your fingers. And that's just for a start. Why, what do we have here?" Brompton took Rawlins by the chin and forced his head up. "This young fellow is crying again. I always thought you weren't Alcott material, Rawlins. Alcott boys never cry, right?"

Howes and Maguire nodded agreement in mock solemnity.

"And this young fellow is crying, even though no one's doing a thing to him. We're just having a talk, right?"

Howes and Maguire nodded again.

"Now if somebody ever really *did* anything to him," Brompton said as he grabbed Rawlins by the hand and began to push the smaller boy's index finger back and back. Rawlins gasped, and Brompton stopped. "If somebody ever really *did* anything to him, I'll bet he'd pass out right on the spot. Anybody want to take that bet?"

Howes and Maguire, in unison, shook their heads from side to side.

"Now listen," Brompton commanded, looking directly into Rawlins' eyes until Rawlins desperately turned his head away. "Listen good. If you say it was us, you will never be safe again for the rest of your life. You will never know when we're coming, but sooner or later, we'll get you. Right?"

Howes and Maguire nodded vigorously, menacingly.

"If you say it was us," Brompton dug his fingers into the back of Tim's neck, "you will have *had* it. Understand?"

"What makes you so sure that the headmaster will

believe his own son is a crook?" Maguire said to Brompton.

"What evidence is there that Sam is *not* a crook?" Brompton smiled in anticipation of what was to come. "Here we have this poor young soul"—he patted Rawlins on the head—"finally breaking free of that evil Sam by having the courage to turn him in to his own father."

"I don't know." Maguire rubbed his upper lip.

"Tell me," Brompton demanded, "what's the first thing that comes into your head when you hear the name 'Sam'?"

"Trouble," Maguire answered. "That kid is always getting into trouble. You never know where he's going to screw up next. Even the seniors know his reputation. But trouble's one thing, stealing's another."

"You ever been in trouble?" Brompton asked Rawlins, who had his hands over his head and had sunk almost to his knees in the corner of the doorway.

"No," Rawlins said in a voice that could barely be heard. "Not until now."

"See," Brompton said. "Here's a boy with an unblemished record who has been forced into a life of crime by a known troublemaker. And when that troublemaker—*to save his own skin*—names *us* as the true culprits, who's going to believe him?"

"I won't do it! I won't!" Rawlins' voice was now so hoarse it hurt him to speak.

"Yes, you will," Fred Brompton said, punching him again in the stomach. "When the time comes, you'll think of Number One, just like everybody else does. Come on," Brompton said to Howes and Maguire, "this brave little fellow knows what he has to do."

The three older boys left the doorway. Rawlins was sitting on the ground in a corner of the doorway, his head between his knees. He heard them laughing as they went up the street. He wished that he was dead.

10

The next morning, Rawlins, unable to eat breakfast, started off to school early.

Uptown, Blake Edwards was on a subway train. Downtown, Sam and Benjy met at their usual corner and began to walk to the subway. Across town, Fat Jake was also on his way, his book bag on his shoulder. Inside it there was a large, handsome lunch box.

Fat Jake carried the lunch box to school despite the rule against students' bringing food into the building. He kept it in his locker, which now was secured by two new locks. The lunch box made it possible for Jake to be more selective in deciding which parts of the school lunch he would eat. And some days Jake would consume all the school lunch and all the supplementary delights stashed in his locker to meet the needs of a growing boy.

Jake would have much preferred being able to display the lunch box openly because it was one of a kind, made for him by his father. Round rather than square, it had separate compartments for sandwiches, hard-boiled eggs, cookies, fruits, and candy. And a place for two thermos bottles—one for milk, the other for Coke. "Be careful with it," his father had told him. "Tin isn't iron."

Each morning, Jake carefully packed the lunch box, it being too vital a job to delegate to his mother. And each morning, he put all his books and all but one of his notebooks into his book bag before gently placing the lunch box on top of them. Then he put a large loose-leaf notebook over the lunch box.

This morning, as Jake neared school, Blake ran up to him shouting, "Look! Look!" and pointing to the sky. As Jake looked up, Sam swooped by, grabbed the loose-leaf notebook from Jake's bag, saw the lunch box underneath, let the notebook drop and ran off with the lunch box instead. As he tossed it to Blake, Benjy appeared, just in time to take a lateral pass from Blake. Sam dropped back behind Jake as Benjy threw the lunch box over Jake's head. Sam caught it just before it hit the ground. Jake, roaring with rage, kept throwing up his hands in a desperate attempt to intercept the lunch box.

"What's going on here?" Mr. Kozodoy, his arms folded, his foot tapping, looked down from the door of the school. "Stop it!" he shouted.

Sam, about to throw a pass to Benjy, was distracted by Mr. Kozodoy's bellow and threw the lunch box way past Benjy into the street, where it landed just in time to be crushed by a truck.

Stunned, Jake froze, arms halfway up, mouth open. Sam, shaking his head, looked at the destroyed lunch box, walked over to Jake, and said, "Hey, I'm sorry. We were just horsing around."

"Yeah," Blake said sadly. Benjy nodded.

There was no answer. Jake picked up his book bag, and slowly, very slowly walked up the stairs.

"Listen," Sam said, running after him, "we'll buy you a new lunch box. A bigger one, a better one."

Jake stared at Sam. "You can't."

"Sure we can," Sam said. "We'll buy you the best lunch box there is."

"You can't." Jake turned his back on Sam.

"Damn," Sam said to Benjy. "We should have gotten that truck's license number. We could have sued him for another lunch box."

"No, you couldn't," Blake said. "It wasn't his fault."

Sam's shoulders slumped and he muttered, "Yeah, I'd forgotten that. Still, a driver ought to know enough to stop when a lunch box lands in front of him."

"Sure," Benjy said, "it happens every day."

"Aw, look," Sam said, turning to him, "I feel bad enough already."

"And it wasn't even your lunch box," Blake said sardonically.

"Hey, you're all acting as if I was the only one responsible for what happened," Sam said with a frown. "I wasn't tossing that lunch box just to myself, you know."

"Well," Benjy said, "you're the one who grabbed it out of his book bag to start with."

"Now listen—" Sam began angrily.

"No, you listen." Mr. Kozodoy had come down the

steps. "Each of you will serve two hours' detention every day for a week."

"But I already got detention," Sam said.

"I am well aware of that," Mr. Kozodoy said. "You will begin serving detention for *this* episode as soon as your detention for the lunchroom episode is finished."

"Oh, Jesus." Sam threw his book bag to the ground.

"That's another day of detention," Mr. Kozodoy said, "for swearing."

"That's not swearing," Sam protested.

"I decide what swearing is," said Mr. Kozodoy as he began to ascend the stairs.

At the moment Fat Jake's lunch box was being flattened by the truck, Tim Rawlins was rubbing his fingers nervously as he stood in front of the headmaster's desk.

"Well, what have you decided?" the headmaster asked.

There was no response.

The headmaster leaned forward. "You do remember that if you refuse to tell me the names of those boys who *made* you steal, as you put it yesterday, you will be expelled."

Rawlins nodded.

"Do you want to do that to your parents, let alone to yourself?"

Tim closed his eyes. "No, sir."

"Let me also underline what I told you yesterday about your fear of retaliation by those thugs. I shall make it inescapably clear to them that *any* retaliation, even just a verbal threat, will instantly result in my bringing formal charges against them with the police."

"You're going to keep them in the school?" Rawlins was astonished.

"No," the headmaster answered. "If the boys you name are proved guilty, they will be expelled. But I will retain the proof of what they have done, and after I talk to them, Rawlins, I can guarantee you they will not bother you again."

Rawlins very much wanted to believe the headmaster but could not get last night's terrifying encounter out of his mind.

"Who *are* they?" The headmaster raised his voice. Rawlins took a deep breath, but was silent.

"Well, you leave me no choice. You are expelled. I shall arrange a meeting with your parents to explain why I had to take this drastic action."

"No, wait." Rawlins clenched and unclenched his hands. "Please wait."

"I am waiting," the headmaster said.

Rawlins again saw himself trapped in the corner of the doorway with Brompton, Howes, and Maguire looming over him. Nothing will keep them away from me, Rawlins thought, nothing.

"I am still waiting," the headmaster said.

"It wasn't a 'they,' sir." Rawlins' voice was so soft that the headmaster had to strain to make out what he was saying. "It was one person."

"Whose name is—"

"I—I don't know." Rawlins was trying desperately to find a way out. "I never saw him. He—he always wears a mask when he appears."

"Oh, come on," the headmaster said, looking at his

watch. "Next you'll tell me he wears a black cowboy hat. What do you take me for? Now listen"—the headmaster walked over to Rawlins and held his watch next to the boy's ear—"you have sixty seconds to decide whether you are to be expelled."

Keeping the watch next to Rawlins' ear, the headmaster looked down at the most miserable boy he had ever seen. "Forty seconds." The headmaster bent down to look at the watch. "Thirty-nine, thirty-eight, thirty-seven, thirty-six, thirty-five, thirty—"

"Stop. Please stop it." Rawlins' head was so low that his chin touched his chest. "It—it's Sam."

Startled, the headmaster drew his hand back. "That's absurd. Sam could never be part of anything like this. It's impossible."

Rawlins looked at the floor and said nothing.

"You can't stop there." The headmaster twisted a paper clip out of shape. "I want the details."

"There's nothing else," Rawlins said mournfully.

The headmaster started pacing the floor. "Oh, no, I want to know how long this has been going on. I want to know why you didn't come to me as soon as it started. I want to know a great many things."

"You said I just had to name somebody," Rawlins said in a monotone. "You didn't say anything about details."

"Of course I meant details." The headmaster stopped in front of Rawlins. "You can't bring this serious a charge against a boy, any boy, and just give his name."

"Sir," Rawlins said, "I think I am going to be sick." And he threw up on the arm of a leather chair and on the green carpet.

"O God," the headmaster said, turning his head away. He felt he might vomit, too. "Very well, go to the nurse. And then come back as soon as she's through with you."

"Please, sir, can't it wait until tomorrow? I feel awful."

"As well you should," the headmaster said fiercely. "All right, eight thirty tomorrow morning. And tell your parents to come. Never mind, I'll telephone them."

"But you said that I wouldn't be expelled if I told," Rawlins whimpered.

"So I did," the headmaster acknowledged. "But I did not say I would not suspend you. We shall see about that tomorrow morning. And remember, I want the details, *all* the details."

Rawlins barely nodded as he turned around and left the headmaster's office. Outside, he leaned against the wall, nausea swelling inside him again.

"O.K., Rawlins, how did it go?" Brompton asked. e, Howes, and Maguire had materialized in front f Tim.

"I did what you said." Rawlins lowered his head and threw up on Brompton's shoes.

11

The first thing Sam saw when he came into the headmaster's office ten minutes later was one of the school handymen briskly moving a mop over a patch of the green carpet. Beside him was a bucket and a small pile of rags.

Sam's father was standing by the window, looking out.

"God," Sam said, "what's that smell? Ech! It's like someone threw up."

"You got it," the handyman said. "You got a smart boy." He turned to grin at the headmaster.

The headmaster looked at the handyman coldly. "O.K.," he said. "That's good enough. Thank you."

The man shrugged, picked up the pail and the rags and the mop, and left the office.

"Sit down," Sam's father said.

"O.K." Sam uneasily took the chair nearest the desk. "How come you had to see me right now?"

"I have sent for you, Sam, as an Alcott student," his father said. "This is a school matter. Do you understand?"

"Yeah."

"The word is *yes*," the headmaster said.

"O.K. Yes, *sir!*"

"Twice now, you have told me you know nothing —nothing at all—about the stealing that has been going on here. Is that still your story?"

Sam was knocking on the wooden armrest of the chair with his knuckles.

"Stop that!" the headmaster said. "It's irritating."

"Yes, *sir!*"

"Sam, I don't think you are fully aware of the seriousness of this conversation. Rawlins was in here a few minutes ago."

"Yeah?" Sam began to feel apprehensive. "So?"

"I ask you again, is it still your story that you know nothing about Rawlins' involvement in the stealing?"

"I don't have any story." Sam changed his position on the chair. "Except maybe what somebody told me."

"Somebody who?" the headmaster snapped.

"Hey," Sam said, "what is this? I'm your son, remember?"

"I know that all too well," the headmaster said frostily. "I also know that you are an Alcott student as well as my son. And as an Alcott student, you will not be treated any differently from anyone else."

After a moment's pause, his father's voice softened. "Sam, stop playing games with me. Please. I want to know exactly what part you have played in this."

"What part!" Sam was startled. "I didn't have *any* part in it."

"All right," the headmaster said, "I'll ask you again. *Who* told you *what* about the stealing?"

"Look," Sam said, "I made a promise not to tell *anybody*."

"You are saying to me," the headmaster said as he began hitting the desk with his index finger in a regular, drumming beat—a sure sign, Sam knew, his father was angry—"that you had knowledge of criminal activity in this school and you not only withheld that knowledge from me but you also *lied* and said you knew nothing about it. Is that what you're saying?"

Sam was now wiggling uncomfortably in his chair. "Yes, if that's the way you want to put it. I mean, I didn't know anything at all, I really didn't, and then this boy told me something and made me swear not to repeat it. And like you've told me, a man is as good as his word."

The headmaster slapped his hand on the desk. "I never told you that it is right to conceal criminal behavior, no matter what kind of promise of silence has been made."

"I guess I didn't hear that part." Sam tried a smile. "I'll have to think about that."

His father did not smile back. "You don't have time to think about it. It is essential that I know *now*."

Sam rubbed his chin, stuck a finger in his ear, and

scratched his head. "First let me talk to the boy I made the promise to. I owe him that."

"Was that boy Tim Rawlins?" the headmaster said.

"I can't say."

"I can say it for you," the headmaster said.

Sam relaxed. "You mean he's told you that he came to me for help."

"No, that is not what he told me. This morning he told me that *you* are the boy who has been forcing him to steal so that he can hand the money over to *you*."

Sam felt as if somebody had just punched him hard in the stomach. He shook his head hard from side to side before he could speak.

"Me? *Me?*" Sam squeaked. "That's impossible. It's not true. Rawlins couldn't have told you that."

"He did." The headmaster looked closely at his son.

"But that's crazy. He told me who was shaking him down—Brompton, Howes, and Maguire. Not Marty Brompton on the football team, but his brother, Fred."

"He only gave me *your* name," the headmaster said.

Sam shot out of the chair and stood in front of his father. "And you believe it! You really believe it! I can tell. You really believe that I could do something scrimy like that."

"I am informing you," the headmaster said, looking past Sam, "of the charges that have been made against you, and I am giving you an opportunity to answer those charges."

"See? See? I was right." Sam's voice cracked again.

"You're talking to me as if I wasn't even your son, but some kind of criminal."

"Sam," his father said softly. "I have given you every opportunity to tell me the truth. Each time, you have not told me the truth." The headmaster sighed, turned away from Sam, and then turned back. "I have to remind you again that every boy in this school gets treated fairly. The same standards of honesty and of decent behavior apply equally to all the boys, including you. I would have thought that was very clear to you by now."

"I understand that." Sam was hopping up and down. "But you're treating me as if you've already decided I'm guilty. Is *that* fair?"

"I am treating you as I would any boy in your position."

"My *position!* See! See!" Sam was finding it hard to breathe. "You take anybody's word against mine. You hate me! Well, I hate you!" He rushed toward the door.

"Come back here!" the headmaster shouted. "We're not through yet."

"Oh, yes we are," Sam shouted back.

The headmaster started after his son, stopped as the door slammed, walked slowly to his desk, sat down, and stared out the window through the tears in his eyes.

12

Mr. Kozodoy practically skipped into the teachers' lounge. "Have you heard?"

Miss Sullivan had never seen him so pleased. In fact, she thought, she had never seen him really pleased before, except for the day the headmaster broke his ankle falling downstairs in pursuit of a runaway gerbil.

"What haven't we heard?" Miss Saperstein was sitting on the couch, leafing through a magazine.

"Not only has the thief been caught," Mr. Kozodoy paused for effect, "but the *master* thief has also been caught."

"You mean whoever was preying on poor little Rawlins?" Miss Sullivan asked. "I couldn't believe that shy little child would steal unless someone had frightened him into it."

"An excellent guess." Mr. Kozodoy took his time filling a cup with coffee. "I happened to be outside the headmaster's office a few minutes ago and I heard him interrogating the real criminal, who suddenly ran out of the office and down the stairs. It was obviously a desperate attempt at escape."

"O.K.," Miss Saperstein said, "you've had your fun. Who is the master thief?"

"Sam." Mr. Kozodoy seemed to smack his lips together as he repeated, "Sam."

"Oh, no!" Miss Sullivan exclaimed. "That's not possible."

"Possible or not," Mr. Kozodoy said, smiling, "that wretched boy has finally been found out."

"Just a minute," Miss Saperstein said as she put down her cup of coffee. "Did you hear Sam admit he was the one?"

Mr. Kozodoy carefully poured himself another cup. "My dear, his running out of his father's office *is* his admission of guilt."

"Not necessarily," Miss Sullivan said. "Sam has a tendency to do something, anything, headlong when he feels everything's going against him through no fault of his own."

"Through no fault of his own that he'll admit to," Miss Saperstein corrected. "Once everything gets sorted out, you usually find that Sam has contributed greatly to whatever mess he's in."

"Yes," Miss Sullivan agreed. "But stealing is *so* unlike Sam, even at his very worst. I don't think I would really believe that boy was a thief even if I caught him in the act."

"I'm sorry to hear that," Mr. Kozodoy said with

annoyance. "I would think that teachers, of all people, should be able to distinguish between reality and fantasy. I must also remind you of the incident in the gym yesterday when Sam would not allow his locker to be searched."

"Hmmm, we never did find out," Miss Sullivan said as if only to herself, "who stole the book money and the baseball cards in our homeroom."

"Oh, yes," Miss Saperstein said, lighting a cigarette. "I heard that alarmingly fat boy, Jake, complaining bitterly in the lunchroom yesterday about his missing baseball cards. By the way, he really is an awful nuisance, the way he complains all the time."

"No, it's not that simple," Miss Sullivan said. "Jake really is a rather decent boy, but he gets teased so often that he's always on edge. And that leads to his eating all the more and that leads to his being teased all the more. It's my fault and yours, too." She turned to Miss Saperstein. "We should come down much harder on the way the other boys treat Jake. You know, I swear that children are much less kind to each other than when I started teaching fifteen or so years ago."

"Not so," Mr. Kozodoy said sharply. "From time immemorial, children have been cruel to each other. Children are savages, and our job, alas, is to civilize them as best we can, given their basically mean, vicious nature."

"No," Miss Saperstein shook her head. "No, it's not the same as it used to be. Children were much better behaved when I started to teach. I seriously think we ought to have a required course for them to learn how to get along with each other."

"And who among us is sufficiently masochistic to teach such a course?" Mr. Kozodoy asked.

"I strongly doubt," Miss Sullivan said, peering at Kozodoy through her glasses, "that such a course would work no matter who taught it. Children learn far more from their families than from us about how to behave. Fear of consequences can keep most of them reasonably orderly here in school, but we can't teach them kindness and generosity. That they learn at home, and if it's not there at home, then they never really learn it."

"I'm not so sure of that," Miss Saperstein said. "They also pick up ways of behaving, good and bad, from their teachers."

"Well, I am in no way responsible for how that awful Sam acts," Mr. Kozodoy insisted. "Nor even, I suspect, is the headmaster. Some people are just born rotten, and Sam is a definite case in point. All children need to be civilized, but that boy needs to be put in a cage. I really cannot understand your refusal to face the facts, the unavoidable facts, about that appalling, disgusting boy." Mr. Kozodoy moved toward the door.

"It's a pity," Miss Sullivan said, "that you didn't live in that period of history in which your true gifts would have been most fully recognized."

"And what period of history was that?" Mr. Kozodoy asked.

"The Inquisition," Miss Sullivan said. Miss Saperstein giggled.

"How clever, how very clever," said Mr. Kozodoy. "Please do not invite me to the canonization ceremony for Saint Samuel." Leaving the room, he slammed the door.

Sam marched down the stairs, past the guard.

"Hey!" the guard said. "Wait a minute. You know the rules—"

"The rules are for Alcott boys," Sam said over his shoulder. "I'm not one of them anymore."

"Hey!" another voice called. Sam stopped. "Where are you going?" Benjy asked. Blake was with him.

"My man," Blake said to the guard, "we are going to confer briefly out there in the cool, brisk, stimulating air, and you have my word that we will be within call."

"Don't you 'my man' me," the guard said testily. "The rules are the rules, and they apply to you too, smart-ass."

"Do you talk to other Alcott students that way?" Blake asked accusingly.

"When they sass me, young fellow, when they sass me." The guard rose from his chair and put his face close to Blake's. "I don't take no crap from *nobody*, you hear? I do my job, but I don't eat no shit, you understand?"

"O.K.," Blake smiled. "You are my man. Honest, we're going to stay right near the door."

"So long as I can see you," the guard said, slightly mollified. "I ain't going to report you. But don't you play me for a fool."

"No way," Blake said. "I know better than that."

"Hey," Benjy said as he and Blake caught up with Sam outside, "it's all over the damn school—that little rat Rawlins saying you're the one who put him up to stealing. Your father doesn't believe that, does he?"

Sam blinked his eyes fast so as not to cry. "Yes, he does. He sure does."

"What the hell are you going to do?" Blake asked.

"Well, I'm not staying here, I'll tell you that. I've had it with this school, and I've had it with its headmaster."

"For Chrissakes, you idiot," Benjy said. "If you just walk out, it'll look like Rawlins fingered you right."

"I don't give a damn," Sam muttered. "Let anybody think what they want to. The hell with them. The hell with all of them. I'm going my own way."

"Terrific," Blake said. "You're going your own way, huh? Like where? And with *what?*"

"I got twenty-four dollars at home," Sam said defiantly.

Blake looked at Benjy. "Terrific. That should be enough to get him a *long* way away. Yes, sir, he can go clear to Philadelphia on that. And then what?" Blake turned to Sam.

"I don't know." Sam was taking a stance familiar to his friends—that of a small, unyielding bull.

"Come off it," Benjy said, pleading. "You got to face it sooner or later and since you *know* it wasn't you, the sooner the better."

"And maybe now you'll tell us what you *do* know," Blake said to Sam. "I figured all along you knew something about that Rawlins kid."

"Yeah," Sam said. "He told me that Brompton, Howes, and Maguire were shaking him down, and he swore me not to tell."

"Those goddamn goons," Benjy said. "O.K.," he looked at Blake, "we'll get something on them."

"How do you propose to do that?" Blake asked. "You and me and Sam gonna beat it out of them?"

A fifth-grader stopped at the guard's desk, showed him an envelope, and was waved past. The guard's finger pointed to Sam. The boy came up to Sam and handed him a letter. "From the headmaster," the boy said, and walked back into the school.

Blake and Benjy looked at each other. "What the hell—" Benjy began.

Sam opened the letter, read it, and his face twisted in anger and hurt, handed the letter to Benjy, who read it aloud: " 'You are instructed to be in my office promptly at eight thirty tomorrow morning. Mr. Timothy Rawlins will also be there.' And he signs it," Benjy exclaimed in astonishment, " 'Carl Davidson, Headmaster.' Jesus, that's some father you've got."

"Oh," Sam scuffed his feet, "he *is* the headmaster, right? I mean, what do you expect? 'Dear Sam, please come see me tomorrow to get thrown out of Alcott? Love, Dad.' "

"Yeah, but he didn't have to have a *letter* delivered to you," Benjy said. "He could have told you at home tonight."

"Strange cat," Blake said. "But then I wouldn't know about fathers who are headmasters."

Sam read the letter again and stuffed it in his pocket.

"Well," Blake said, "we got to start working on this case—fast."

"Blake," Sam spoke in a low voice. "This isn't television. I go up there tomorrow morning and it's just me and Rawlins. His word against mine."

"So?" Benjy said. "Your father knows you, damn it. He knows you wouldn't do something like that."

"It's the headmaster I'll be talking to tomorrow," Sam said.

"I don't understand that," Blake said. "I don't understand that at all. No way anybody can make me understand that. Anyway," he said to Benjy, "we got to find that Rawlins."

"Wait a minute," Benjy said, "I saw him leave the school about a half hour ago."

They raced back to the guard's desk. "You see a skinny kid, fifth-grader named Rawlins, go out?" Blake asked the guard.

"Yeah," the guard looked at an open notebook in front of him. "He came down a while ago with a note from the headmaster's secretary. The kid was sick, had to go home."

The three boys moved away from the desk. "Then we got to go home after him," Blake whispered.

"No," Benjy said. "We can't just barge in there and force it out of him with his mother there and all. And you can bet he's going to *stay* home until tomorrow morning."

"We could call him," Blake suggested.

"Yeah," Benjy thought for a moment. "There's not much you can do over the phone when a kid is more afraid of somebody else than he is of you. But we can try. Sam, why don't you call him, and we'll be standing by?"

"I'm not going to beg that little worm for anything," Sam said.

"Oh, for God's sake," Blake hissed. "This is no time for that pride crap. You're not begging him. You're telling him he got you into this. You kept your dumb word to him, and you're telling him he damn well better get you out of it."

"No," Sam said. "If Rawlins is so scared he'd lie about me to my father, all I'll get from him is whimpers and 'sorry, sorry, sorry.' No, that fink is a lost cause."

Sam stopped and looked down at the pavement. "Now do you see what I mean? Any way you look at it, I got to leave."

Benjy put his hand on Sam's arm. "We'll figure out something. You run away, you have to come back. It makes no sense, Sam. Don't do anything like that yet. We have until tomorrow morning."

Sam bit his lip. "O.K., I'll think about it."

Blake looked at Benjy glumly. "Like the boy said, this isn't a television script." There was silence. "But there's gotta be some way to turn this around."

The three boys walked back into the school.

"All right, gentlemen," the guard said, smiling. "You kept your word."

"That's the whole goddamn trouble," Blake said, in passing. Puzzled, the guard stared at Blake.

"Nothing to do with you, my man," Blake said. "Nothing to do with you."

Watching the three boys trudge up the stairs, the guard shook his head in perplexity.

13

"I am going to call the police," Mrs. Davidson said. "Sam's been late to dinner before, but never *this* late."

"He'll be home for supper." Her husband was sitting at the kitchen table sipping from a glass of Scotch and water.

"What makes you so damn sure?" his wife asked. "After the way you treated him today."

"I tell you again, I was not one bit harder on Sam than I would have been on any boy under suspicion."

"Under suspicion, indeed!" Liz Davidson said derisively. "First of all, Sam isn't *any* boy, he's your son, damn it. It's stupid to try to pretend, as you have so mulishly tried to pretend all these years, that once Sam is in school, he's not your son, he's just any boy. That's so stupid, stupid, *stupid*!"

"You may have a point," the headmaster said slowly. "Maybe I will send him to another school next year. His being at Alcott does put too much pressure on him, and I suppose, on me too."

"Damn straight," his wife said.

"But for now"—the headmaster stared at his drink—"we've got to clean up this stealing mèss."

"It's not his mess, it's your mess," Liz Davidson said furiously.

"I'm home." A subdued Sam walked into the kitchen. "You were talking so loud I guess you didn't hear me come in." He looked at his father. "I got your letter."

"*What* letter?" Mrs. Davidson's eyes widened.

"To report to the headmaster at eight thirty tomorrow morning so he can tell whether Rawlins or me is lying," Sam said.

"Whether Rawlins or I," his mother corrected him. Then she turned to her husband. "You sent him a letter! Have you gone crazy? Have you turned into Captain Bligh?"

"It is the regular procedure to inform, in writing, any boy facing charges when he must defend himself and who his accuser is. Damn it, there has to be a statement of the charges, too. I didn't put that in."

"You *are* crazy," his wife said. "You've lost your marbles. 'Any boy facing charges,'" she mimicked her husband. "My God, if I were teaching at your damn school, would you write *me* a letter, *including* the damn charges?"

"Under certain circumstances," her husband said, embarrassed, "I would have to."

"Stubborn! Stubborn! *Stub-born!* You always have

to do things your way—no matter what. It's clear to me where Sam gets that from."

Sam looked at his mother. "You think I was shaking Rawlins down, too, huh?"

"I did not *say* that." His mother lit a cigarette with shaking hands. "I was talking about bullheadedness, not about being a bully." Turning to her husband, she added, "You are driving *me* crazy." She looked to her son. "Of course, I don't believe Rawlins is telling the truth. And neither does your father."

"I'll hear both sides tomorrow," the headmaster said.

"Goddamn!" Liz Davidson grabbed a glass from the sink, threw it wide at her husband, and watched it smash on the floor, and walked swiftly to her room.

Father and son looked at each other, and said nothing. Mr. Davidson took out a broom and a dustpan and started to sweep up the broken glass.

"Mom says that won't get it all," Sam observed. "You got to take some paper towels, dampen them, and then pick up the littlest pieces of glass with the paper towels."

"Thanks," his father said, going to the holder over the sink, and unrolling some paper towels.

Sam walked to his room, closed the door, and turned on his radio.

After two hours alone in his study, Mr. Davidson got up to go to bed. The bedroom was dark when he walked in.

"I'm not asleep." His wife's voice came from the bed. "Have you spoken to Sam?"

"No. I don't seem to have very much luck speaking

to Sam. God knows, Liz, I have asked and asked him to tell me what's going on."

Liz Davidson switched on the lamp next to her side of the bed and sat up. "You listen to me. I am going to ask you a question. I am asking you as your wife and as Sam's mother. Don't give me any of your headmaster rigmarole. *Do you believe Sam forced that boy to steal?* I didn't think I'd have to ask that, but now I see I do."

"No, no." Her husband sat down on the bed. "Of course I don't believe that. No more than I'd believe that *you* would shoplift or forge a check. My God, you can't live with someone over a period of years and not know what he's capable of doing and what he's not capable of doing. You know as well as I do that Sam can be one hell of a pain in the ass, but he's essentially a good kid, a very good kid."

"Then why don't you tell him that?"

"You still don't understand," her husband said. "How would you feel if Tim Rawlins' father were the headmaster and were telling Tim right now, 'Son, I know you're innocent, and tomorrow we'll get that liar Sam'?"

"Do you want to know how I'd feel?" his wife said angrily. "Do you really want to know how I'd feel? I'd feel that man was *human,* that's how I'd feel."

The headmaster put his hand over his eyes. "It's not that simple, Liz. A charge has been made against the boy. Somehow it's already all over the school that Rawlins has accused Sam. I don't know how it leaked, but I'm not surprised. That sort of news travels faster than any news that might make somebody feel good. Though, come to think of it, that is precisely the kind of news that does make a lot of people feel good. Anyway, Sam has to be *wholly* exonerated."

"Who is he, Caesar's wife?" His wife glared at him.

"Listen, Liz, for God's sake, listen!" The headmaster got up from the bed. "The boy has been accused, everyone knows about it, and the only way in which this—this shadow is not going to follow Sam through the rest of his school days and maybe long after is for the whole damn lie to be totally, unanswerably exposed."

The headmaster was pacing back and forth now. "And that means *believably* exposed. The fact, for instance, that I'm his father means that I shouldn't be the only one to hear and judge the evidence. Tomorrow morning, along with Sam and Rawlins, there'll be Tom McEvoy, representing the deans, and Neil Kozodoy, representing the faculty. They'll witness and participate in the whole process."

"Kozodoy!" Liz Davidson screwed up her nose as if she were smelling a river polluted beyond all redemption. "That sour, suspicious, envious man. You *know* how he'd love to have your job. I can't even understand why you keep him in the school, but to choose *him* to be on a jury judging your own son—"

"I keep him in the school," the headmaster said, "because he's a damn good teacher, and also because he's a conservative—a testy, intelligent conservative who's a fine debater. The boys need exposure to that kind of viewpoint and to that kind of temperament."

"I'd rather you had Bill Buckley on the faculty," his wife said.

"Can't afford him. But Liz, stop and think. Don't you see the value of having Kozodoy on the jury, as you put it? Once *he* sees, and acknowledges, that Sam is innocent, it'll all be over. The shadow will be gone."

"It seems to me," Liz Davidson said forcefully, "that you're taking a hell of a chance when it's *our son* who's at stake, or rather at the stake. If you turn out to be wrong, I will never speak to you again. Never."

Her husband stopped pacing. "Perhaps I have more faith in Sam than you have. There's no way anyone can prove that boy guilty of this kind of disgusting behavior. Absolutely no way."

"Then why don't you tell him that *tonight?*" his wife demanded.

"Sam didn't level with *me*."

"O God!" Liz Davidson snapped off the light. "There's part of you that is still a child—an obnoxious, stuffy prig of a child. Good night!"

"The thing of it really is," the headmaster persisted, "I don't want Sam going in there tomorrow looking confident. And he would look confident if I assured him tonight that I know he's not guilty. If Sam goes in cocky, the whole thing will look as if it's been rigged."

"Good *night!*" his wife roared.

As he closed the door to the bedroom, the headmaster heard his wife call after him, "*Prig. Stuffy prig. Stupid, stuffy prig.*"

He went down the hall and stood outside Sam's door. He saw that the light was off, but he could hear the radio. He was about to knock, but dropped his hand and continued down the hall to his study.

At the foot of one of the bookcases was a deep drawer from which the headmaster took out a bottle of Scotch and a glass. He felt inside the ice bucket, but there was only water. Shrugging, the headmaster poured a sizable shot of Scotch into the glass, downed it, and opened his briefcase. Somehow, he could not bring himself to take out any of the work he had brought home. He shut the briefcase and looked at the bottle. Then he turned off the light, went into the hall, took his coat out of the closet, and opened the front door.

"I'm going to take a walk," the headmaster announced to no one. "A long walk."

14

"C'mere," Blake said as he spotted Benjy in the school corridor before classes started the next morning. Benjy, looking desolate, slowly walked over.

"What the hell's the matter with you?" Blake asked.

"I thought you were Sam's friend," Benjy said accusingly. "The matter with me is we said we'd help him, and I haven't been able to think of a damn thing. Nothing. And in ten minutes, Sam's going into his father's office. He's going to his execution is where he's going. What are you looking so cheerful about?"

"I got a plan," Blake said, grabbing Benjy's arm. "But we got to move fast. Come on."

"Come on where?"

"I'll tell you as we go. We got to catch a fish. A little fish, but an important fish."

* * *

The headmaster, Mr. McEvoy, Mr. Kozodoy, and Sam were waiting in the headmaster's office in awkward silence. Sam sneezed, thereby becoming the focus of attention, all the more so as he hunted through his pants pockets and then his jacket pockets and then his shirt pocket for something to wipe his nose with.

"Here," the headmaster said in exasperation as he handed his own handkerchief to his son. "How many times have I told you to carry a handkerchief or some Kleenex with you?"

Sam wiped his nose, snuffled, and started to hand back the handkerchief. "Thanks."

"Never mind 'thanks,'" the headmaster said. "Blow your nose. And I mean really blow it."

Sam followed instructions; everyone else in the room raptly watched him blow his nose hard. When he was through, there was silence again. Sam felt a strong urge to fart, but restrained himself. The headmaster stared vacantly out the window. Mr. McEvoy, the head of the middle school, looked fixedly at the bookshelves opposite the headmaster's desk. Mr. Kozodoy, a faint smile on his face, stared at Sam.

At last there was a knock.

"Come in," the headmaster said.

Tim Rawlins opened the door slowly and stopped when he saw that the headmaster was not alone. Rawlins' eyes took in the faculty members and then Sam. He stepped in, shivering slightly, and quickly turned to the headmaster, who wasted no time on preliminaries.

"Would you repeat what you told me yesterday about why you were stealing?"

Rawlins closed his eyes for a moment, coughed, coughed again, and still did not speak.

"We are waiting."

"I—I had to steal," Rawlins said in a barely audible voice, "because I had to give someone six dollars a week."

"Why did you have to give someone six dollars a week?" the headmaster asked.

"Because otherwise they—he—would beat me up." Rawlins looked at the floor.

"Now, Rawlins, to whom did you give that money?"

Rawlins closed his eyes again and twitched. Sam sneezed loudly, sneezed again, and yet again.

Mr. Kozodoy looked suspiciously at Sam. Mr. McEvoy looked curiously at Sam, and the headmaster sighed. Sam blew his nose and looked straight at Rawlins.

"Go on," the headmaster said.

"I had to—to give the money to—"

"Yes?" The three men and Sam leaned forward.

"S-Sam," Rawlins whispered.

Sam jumped up and stood in front of Rawlins, who kept his eyes down. "That's a lie!" Sam shouted. "That's a goddamn lie!"

"He is intimidating the boy," Mr. Kozodoy complained.

"Sit down, Sam," the headmaster ordered.

"Please, Tim." Sam was still standing in front of Rawlins. "You can't do this. You just can't."

Rawlins would not look up.

"Well, now," Mr. Kozodoy said briskly, "there's the proof, the conclusive proof."

The headmaster looked at Mr. McEvoy.

"Sam," Mr. McEvoy said, "I take it that you deny the charge."

"Deny it!" Sam exploded. "Deny it! I sure as hell do deny it, and I'll tell you *why* he's lying."

"Why, Sam?" Mr. McEvoy asked.

"Because he's scared to death of the assholes who *are* making him steal," Sam said indignantly.

"Watch your language," the headmaster said.

Yes, Mr. Kozodoy snickered to himself, what kind of home do you come from, boy?

"Sorry," Sam said. "But what I said is true. He's afraid those three—bast—uh—bums will beat him to a pulp if he tells the truth."

"Is that true?" Mr. McEvoy asked Rawlins.

Rawlins said nothing.

"*Is it true?*" the headmaster pressed Rawlins.

Rawlins bit his lip.

"And I'll tell you who those ass—asses are," Sam was on his feet again. "Brompton, Howes, and Maguire, that's who!"

"Marty Brompton?" Mr. McEvoy shook his head in disbelief.

"No," Sam said, "his piggy younger brother, Fred."

Mr. Kozodoy stood up. "Look here," he said. "This is utterly unfair to those three young men. Here we have a boy"—he stared at Sam—"who has been directly accused of an unconscionable act by Rawlins, and now the accused is becoming the accuser to try to get off the hook. He could have named anybody. Before you continue slandering those three young men, Sam, where's the proof? Where's the proof?"

"Well," McEvoy said, "we actually have no proof against Sam beyond this boy's accusation. It's Sam's word against that of Rawlins here. And now it's Sam's word against the three boys *he* has named. I am assuming they, too, will deny being involved in this. So let's have them in here, and hear what they have to say."

"You are letting this boy turn you around," Mr. Kozodoy said as he pointed to Sam. "Look at the records of Brompton, Howes, and Maguire. Their records are spotless. Then look at his." Mr. Kozodoy's finger was now quite close to Sam's nose and Sam had to exercise great restraint in order not to bite it. "Consider his record. A constant troublemaker, continually fresh to his teachers; a boy who has refused to let his locker be searched immediately after one of his classmates had been robbed. It would be absurd to allow anything he says to cast even the slightest reflection on those three fine young men. I say we have proof enough as to who is really at the disgusting bottom of this."

Sam looked at his father, who was drumming his fingers on his desk.

"Nonetheless," Mr. McEvoy said, "it would greatly ease my mind if we did have a word with the three boys Sam has named. We have to run down every lead we have if we're to be fair."

"I agree," the headmaster said. "And I think it necessary for me to emphasize that although Sam is my—"

Loud voices from just outside the door interrupted the headmaster. "YOU CANNOT GO IN THERE!" shouted his secretary at the top of her voice.

The door opened. Blake, Benjy, and a small, blond fourth-grader carrying a bulging black briefcase came in, closely followed by the headmaster's secretary, who was very agitated.

"I *tried* to stop them, but—"

"Yes, I'm sure you did." The headmaster nodded.

"Sir," Blake said, hauling the fourth-grader behind him as he walked to the front of the headmaster's desk, "this student has something very important to say to you."

Sam, his eyes wide, looked gratefully but with puzzlement at Benjy and Blake.

"It had better be important," the headmaster said sternly, "or all three of you will serve detention for the rest of the month. At least."

Blake pushed the fourth-grader forward. "Tell him," Blake whispered fiercely.

"Sir," the fourth-grader began, tears running down his cheeks. "Sir, three boys bigger than me said they would beat me up if I didn't give them three dollars every week. And that's why this boy," he pointed to Blake, "saw me going through a bunch of desks last week. But I didn't find anything. I didn't take anything from those desks."

"Because you were caught in the act?" Mr. Kozodoy asked acidly.

"Let's try to untangle this," said the headmaster. "Did you steal anything on any *other* day?"

"No, sir," the fourth-grader answered. "That was the first time, and when he"—the boy nodded toward Blake again—"saw me doing it, I got so scared I didn't try it again."

"So where do you get the money you say these boys force you to give them?" the headmaster asked.

"Do I have to answer, sir?" The boy was trying very hard to keep himself in control.

"You certainly do," the headmaster said sternly.

"From home, sir." The fourth-grader started to cry. "From my mother's pocketbook."

"And to whom did you have to give this stolen money?" the headmaster asked.

"To three boys in the upper school, sir. I don't know their names, except for one of them, Brompton. His brother's on the football team."

The dean of the middle school looked at Mr. Kozodoy. "Well, now we shall *certainly* have to speak to those three young men. This is becoming quite confusing."

"It's not at all confusing," Mr. Kozodoy said heatedly. "This is a setup, a trick by those two," he said as he shook his finger at Blake and Benjy, "to rescue their friend. It's like an old movie with the cavalry arriving in the nick of time. Here, I'll show you."

Mr. Kozodoy motioned to the fourth-grader to stand in front of him. "Tell me, young man," he said, "did you come here this morning of your own free will or were you forced to come?"

The boy had stopped crying. His face tightened as he looked toward Blake and Benjy. "Those two—those two," the boy said, "told me they would beat me up if I didn't come here with them."

"You see," Mr. Kozodoy said triumphantly to Mr. McEvoy.

"Sir." The fourth-grader now faced the headmaster. "Sir, this is not a safe school if you're little. You should do something about that."

"You're quite right," the headmaster said. "I am ashamed to admit that you are quite right. And I shall do something about it. But why didn't you come straight to me when those three boys started bothering you?"

"If it was three boys," Mr. Kozodoy interrupted, "and not just one."

"Because," the fourth-grader answered, "they said they'd fix me good if I told. And now, this morning, these two boys said they'd fix me good right then if I *didn't* tell."

"This is getting to be more and more confusing," Mr. McEvoy said.

"And you," the headmaster said angrily to Blake, "why didn't you come to me when you saw this boy going through those desks?"

The fourth-grader looked intently at Blake.

"Well, uh—" Blake began. "I didn't think he'd do it anymore and uh—well, you just heard him say he *didn't* do it anymore."

"That was not your decision to make," the headmaster said. "I want to talk to you later this morning about the responsibilities you have—and have not at all fulfilled in this instance—to this school, to your fellow students, and to yourself."

Blake nodded glumly.

"And both of you," the headmaster said as he looked first at Blake and then at Benjy, "are obviously guilty of threatening this young fellow with a beating this very morning."

"But, sir," Benjy exclaimed, "we did that so the truth would come out. Besides, we were just talking, we wouldn't have touched him."

"So you say," the headmaster said grimly. "I will see you both at ten o'clock."

"Can I go now?" the fourth-grader asked anxiously. "I'm late for class."

"That is the least of your worries," the headmaster answered. "I am going to call your parents, and all of us are going to have a talk about how you have failed *your* responsibility to this school. Until we have that talk, you, young man, are temporarily suspended. My secretary will make arrangements to get you home."

In frustration and fury, the fourth-grader kicked Benjy hard in the shin and tried to get at Blake, but was held back by Benjy, who all the while yelled in pain.

"Damn you, damn you," the small boy cried as he struggled to get free. "Why didn't you let me alone, damn you?"

"That's *all*," the headmaster said in his deepest voice. Benjy let the fourth-grader go, and vigorously rubbed his shin. The smaller boy stuck his tongue out at Blake.

"Where do we go from here?" Mr. McEvoy asked. "I'm not sure I have all this sorted out."

The headmaster ran his hand through his hair, rubbed his nose and said, "I'll have to set up another meeting with Brompton, Howes, and Maguire in attendance."

"If we are still getting at all the facts," Mr. McEvoy asked as he pointed to the fourth-grader, "why should this child be the only one suspended?"

"He is the only boy so far, aside from Rawlins," the headmaster answered, "who has confessed that he has stolen, at home, and has tried to steal here. But you do have a point. I suppose it is unfair at this point for him to be the only one penalized, since I have not taken any action yet against Rawlins."

"Can I go to class then, sir?" the fourth-grader asked hopefully.

"Yes," the headmaster said. "For the time being. All right, go! All of you, go to class!" He waved Blake, Benjy, the fourth-grader, and Sam out of the room.

"My head is spinning," Mr. McEvoy said when the boys had left. "I'm not entirely sure whom to believe at this point. First Rawlins—say, where *is* Rawlins?"

"I'll be damned," the headmaster said. "He must have slipped out while we were all involved with that little fellow with the big briefcase."

"Did Rawlins leave," Mr. McEvoy asked no one in particular, "because that boy's story would show that Rawlins was lying about Sam? Or is it possible that *two* shakedown operations are going on, and Rawlins left because he thought we were done for the time being with the one he knew about?"

"No, that doesn't make sense," the headmaster said. "Sam accused Brompton, Howes, and Maguire by name before that little fellow came in."

"That could have been arranged beforehand," interjected Mr. Kozodoy.

"I must say," Mr. McEvoy said as he scratched his head, "I need some tranquility to figure this all out."

"Tomorrow, *everybody* will be here," the headmaster said, "and we'll get it all figured out. Oh, my! Isn't that the fourth-grader's briefcase on the floor? As if that boy didn't have enough to worry about. I'll take it up to his room."

"I don't quite know what to make of *that* boy," Mr. Kozodoy said.

"He's not much of a puzzle," the headmaster said, smiling slightly. "I think it is safe to say that while that boy has stolen, he is not a thief."

"Now that doesn't make any sense," Mr. Kozodoy said.

"I thought you might find it a little difficult," said the headmaster, carrying the bulging black briefcase to the door. "You'll all excuse me, but that youngster might need something in this right away."

"Neil," Mr. McEvoy said after the headmaster had left, "you were uncharacteristically silent for most of the time. What do you think?"

"I was trying to figure it out," Mr. Kozodoy answered. "Somehow that Sam has found a loophole, or rather his friends have found it for him. But I'll work it out by tomorrow. No kids are going to outwit me."

"I got to say it again," Sam said as he caught up with Benjy and Blake in the corridor later that morning. "That was a great thing you guys did."

"Think nothing of it," Benjy said morosely. "It just cost me two whole weeks on detention and then God knows what. He said he'd review my case after I'm through with detention."

"And I got three goddamn weeks," Blake said, shaking his head in disgust. "*Plus* whatever he decides later. *Plus* what I'll get at home."

"You got the extra week because you didn't turn the kid in when you saw him going through the desks?" Sam asked Blake.

"Cor-rect! You got it. Shee-it, something like this always happens when you butt into something that's none of your business." Blake shoved a stick of gum into his mouth and chewed furiously.

"Look, I'm sorry about this," Sam said. "I'll make it up to both of you somehow."

"Forget it," Benjy said dourly. Suddenly, he laughed. "Hey, Blake, we broke the case! We saw that jus–tice was done. How about that?"

"You can take justice and ram it," Blake said gloomily.

"Anyway," Sam said, "it's not over yet. Those three bastards are sure as hell going to try to lie themselves out of this."

"Well, if you need any help," Blake said as he started down the stairs, "be sure not to let me know about it."

"You don't *mean* that," Benjy said.

Blake turned around, tried not to smile, and failed. "No, I guess I don't," he said. "Yeah, we broke the case! How *about* that?" He punched Sam lightly on the arm. "If it hadn't been for us, young man"—he made his voice as deep as he could—"you would be on your way, right now, to a max-i-mum se-cu-ri-ty prison. And yet our fee, despite all we have done, despite the dangers we have run, despite the penalties we have yet to pay, is very reasonable."

Sam laughed. "What is it?"

"*All* your baseball cards," Blake said.

Sam stopped laughing and nodded. "Well, you're entitled. I'll bring them in tomorrow."

"Come *on*," Benjy said. "Can't you tell when Blake is kidding?"

"But I do owe you guys a lot."

"Listen," Blake said, "what we did for you, you'd do for us. That's what counts. That has nothing to do with *owing*, you know."

"Yeah," Sam said with a grin, "I know."

15

In the headmaster's office the next morning, Tim Rawlins watched as the small, blond-haired fourth-grader, clutching his briefcase, told his story again. This time he pointed at Brompton, Howes, and Maguire—his tormentors.

"The young man is well rehearsed," Mr. Kozodoy said nastily. "Now let us hear from the three boys who have been dragged into this case."

"Well?" The headmaster turned to Brompton, Howes, and Maguire. They were trying as best they could to look both shocked and outraged.

"Sir," Fred Brompton began. "I don't know why this boy is saying these things about us, but I can assure you—"

"I know! I know!" Rawlins cried as he leaped to

his feet. "He's saying those things because they're true." Rawlins turned toward Sam. "I feel terrible about yesterday," he said. "Just terrible."

Sam looked at Rawlins, but said nothing.

Rawlins moved toward the headmaster's desk. "I lied yesterday," he said. "It wasn't Sam at all. It was these three."

"Sir, sir!" Brompton was still trying to look indignant, but Howes and Maguire just looked sick. "Sir, whatever he said to you yesterday, Rawlins is lying *today*. This is some kind of conspiracy to—"

"Do you know this boy?" the headmaster asked Rawlins and pointed to the fourth-grader.

"No, sir," Rawlins answered.

"Do you know this boy?" the headmaster asked the fourth-grader, pointing to Rawlins.

"I've seen him in the corridor, sir, but I don't know him."

"Does that sound like a conspiracy to you, Brompton?" the headmaster asked.

"Sir!" Brompton looked desperately to Howes and Maguire. "There's a terrible misunderstanding here—"

"Hey," the fourth-grader broke in, "there's the pen I got for my birthday." He walked up to Fred Brompton and stretched himself to reach the pen clipped to Brompton's shirt pocket. Brompton drew back, and the boy lowered his hand. He turned to the headmaster. "I was a dollar short last time, so he took the pen instead."

"Sir, this is ridiculous," said Brompton as he unclipped the pen and shoved it into his pocket.

"It's got my initials on it," the fourth-grader said. "S.G. That's for Steve Gorman. Me."

"May I see the pen?" the headmaster asked Brompton.

"Sir, I just happened to find it in the corridor this morning," Brompton said hurriedly. "I haven't had a chance yet to bring it to the lost-and-found room."

"That's possible," Mr. Kozodoy said.

"Not likely," said Mr. McEvoy and he shook his head.

"May I see the pen?" the headmaster repeated.

Brompton gave it to him. The headmaster examined the pen and handed it to the fourth-grader.

"I think we have heard enough lying," the headmaster said to Brompton. Then he asked Howes and Maguire, "What about you? I haven't heard a word out of either of you. Can't you speak for yourselves?"

"You see, sir"—Maguire's voice was higher than usual—"we were just having some fun."

"Yeah," Howes said, gulping. "We weren't going to keep the money."

Brompton looked fiercely at Howes and Maguire. Then, with what he hoped was an ingratiating smile, he moved toward the headmaster. "That's just what it was, sir. We were going to give these boys back their money this week. Tomorrow. It was just a joke." Brompton tried to look sheepish. "I didn't tell you right away this morning, sir, because I thought our little fun might be misinterpreted, as it has been."

The headmaster turned to McEvoy and Kozodoy. "Any questions?" he asked.

The dean of the middle school looked at Brompton. "That is your defense?" he asked. "You have nothing more to say?"

"Except, sir," Brompton said to Mr. McEvoy with

great intensity, "of course we will never ever do anything like this again. We meant no harm, but obviously our intentions were misinterpreted. We've learned our lesson."

"Tell me, Brompton," Mr. McEvoy asked, "how can you possibly say you meant no harm and how can you use the word 'fun' in regard to this, when these boys"—he gestured toward Rawlins and the small fourth-grader—"have so clearly been terrified and, I should add, terrorized?"

"Well"—Brompton seemed to be grabbing for an answer, any answer—"we—we thought their seeming to be scared was like an act on their part. You know, it was a game, and they were pretending to be scared."

Howes and Maguire weakly nodded assent.

The fourth-grader, lugging his briefcase along with him, walked over to Brompton and looked up at him. "That wasn't a game. That wasn't a game when you bent my fingers back until I said I'd get you the money."

The boy turned to Mr. McEvoy. "I wasn't pretending to be scared, sir. I was scared. I was really scared."

"I know you were," said the dean of the middle school.

"Mr. Kozodoy?" the headmaster asked.

Looking at Brompton with distaste, and then at Howes and Maguire with equal distaste, Mr. Kozodoy pursed his lips, and said, "No questions."

"Are you satisfied," the headmaster asked Mr. Kozodoy, "that these three boys are guilty and that Sam was not involved?"

Mr. Kozodoy coughed. "Yes," he said abruptly.

The headmaster turned toward Brompton. "I have a question. How many other boys have you three been shaking down?"

"These were the only two," Brompton answered. Suddenly aware of the wording of the question, he hastened to add, "But we weren't shaking them down. Like I told you, we—"

"Do you prefer the term 'extortion'?" the headmaster asked. "We will see if these boys have been the only two. If there were others, the news of your expulsion should lead them to step forward. And in any case, I will ask that any of your other victims, if there are others, do step forward."

"You said '*expulsion*'?" Brompton seemed to be fighting for air.

"Yes, all of you are expelled, as of this instant."

"But what about due process?" Mr. Kozodoy interrupted. "This has just been a preliminary hearing. They ought to have the right to study the charges further, obtain witnesses for their defense, and perhaps have counsel present."

"I see no purpose in prolonging this any further," the headmaster said. "The evidence is clear, and these three young men have, in effect, confessed. Do *you* have 'due process' problems?" the headmaster asked the dean of the middle school.

"No," Mr. McEvoy said. "These young men have been given a hearing, they have been confronted by the witnesses against them, and, as you say, they have admitted practicing extortion. It is clear to me that the three must be removed from the school."

"You may now collect your books and whatever else

is in your desks and your lockers," the headmaster said to Brompton, Howes, and Maguire. "Then you must leave the school immediately. I shall be in touch with your parents, but I promise you there is no way in which you can come back to this school as long as I am its headmaster. Boys like you are a disease that can infect an entire school unless you are severed from that school. You have corrupted these two youngsters, and perhaps others, by your brutishness. I am sure that you will find some other school, and perhaps a more compassionate headmaster than I. But I cannot stand looking at any of you for one second more. Please leave this office!"

Brompton opened his mouth to say something, but closed it again and joined Howes and Maguire as they left the room.

The headmaster turned to Mr. McEvoy and to Kozodoy. "We have our share of blame too, of course," he said. "How can they have been here so long without our knowing what they were becoming?"

"It's *my* responsibility, actually," Mr. McEvoy said. "Certainly these recent years. I'm supposed to know what's going on in the middle school. But none of those three boys gave the teachers or me any particular trouble so far as behavior was concerned."

"We knew better," Sam said.

"Perhaps," the headmaster said to his son. "But you would never have told Mr. McEvoy that you knew those boys were bullies, that they were mean to the younger kids. Right?"

"Yeah," Sam answered. "I guess you're right."

"You see," the headmaster said to McEvoy and Kozodoy, "there's a whole other life in this school—

what happens between the boys when they are *not* in class—about which we know very little. And the boys do not volunteer information about, let us say, bullies because *omertà* is as sacred a principle to them as it is to the Mafia."

"What's *omertà*, sir?" the fourth-grader asked.

"A vow of silence," said the headmaster. "Among certain organized criminals, there is a pledge never to reveal to outsiders, and certainly not to the police, what goes on inside the criminal world. Even if a member of the criminal group has been badly injured by his colleagues, he will not say a word about it to any outsider. And you too, young man, practice *omertà*. You did not come to me, or to a teacher, as you should have, when those three older boys began to put pressure on you."

"Well," the fourth-grader said, "I mostly didn't say anything because I was scared of what they'd do to me if I told. But also," he looked down, "I don't get the feeling that most of the teachers care about what's going on with us once we leave their classrooms. We're kind of on our own then. And that may be O.K. when you're bigger, but like I said, sir, when you're smaller, this school is not a safe place."

"What do you think we should do about it?" the headmaster asked him.

"I don't know, sir. But you ought to think about it, sir."

"I don't know either," Mr. McEvoy said. "We certainly don't want to plant informers in each class. On the other hand, we physically can't supervise the boys all day long in the corridors, and wherever else they go when they're not in class."

"This doesn't seem to me to be such a terrible problem," Mr. Kozodoy volunteered. "Sure, once in a while things get out of hand—as in this shakedown incident—but boys have to learn how to survive on their own. That's part of their education, too."

The fourth-grader turned to Mr. Kozodoy. "Sir, that's hard to do if you're nine and you have to survive kids who are fifteen and sixteen."

Rawlins nodded agreement.

"I think Steve here," Sam said as he gestured toward the fourth-grader, "is right when he says that most of the time the teachers don't seem to care about us except as students in their classes. It's like they're just here to teach us the thing they teach us, and all they want to know about is how well we're learning that thing. You learn more than subjects in school, though."

"Good lord," Mr. Kozodoy said. "We now have *sixth-graders* coming on as school reformers. If you spent more time on what you're supposed to learn in class, young man, you wouldn't have time to get in trouble with the other boys, including older boys."

"I study hard, sir," the fourth-grader said, "and I don't have time to get in trouble on my own. But in this school, trouble found me."

"O.K.," the headmaster said. "We have a problem. I mean we adults here." He turned to the dean of the middle school and Mr. Kozodoy, "and that is going to be the priority item on our agenda until we can find some sort of solution. We are going to have to ask ourselves some very serious, basic questions. Like, how well do we know *any* boy in this school?"

"Good luck, sir," said the fourth-grader. He spoke with such evident earnestness that even Mr. Kozodoy, briefly, cast a kindly eye on him.

A few minutes later, outside the headmaster's office, Rawlins came up to Sam. "I don't know what else to say except what I already said. It's the worst thing I've ever done in my life—telling that awful lie about you."

Sam stared at him. "What am I supposed to say? Forget it?"

Rawlins looked down at the floor. "I—I hope someday I'll be able to do something to make up for it."

"You want to do something for me?" Sam asked. Rawlins looked up earnestly.

"Just stay the hell away from me." Sam hurried to catch up with the fourth-grader.

"Steve," Sam said to him, "if you run into anything like this again, if anybody puts the muscle on you, let me know. Or if I'm not here next year, you can always go to Benjy and Blake."

The fourth-grader looked solemnly at Sam. "They're the ones who put the muscle on me yesterday."

"Yeah, but that's not like them. They were trying to help me. But believe me, Steve, you can come to us, to any one of us, if you need help."

"I'll think about it," answered the fourth-grader. He walked away clutching his briefcase.

"Where the hell *is* Marty?" Fred Brompton kept repeating to himself as he rushed through the corridors, peering into classrooms; he rushed downstairs, examined the lunchroom, and looked into the gym, where he found his older brother jogging on the otherwise deserted basketball court.

Pushing the door open, Fred Brompton yelled, "Hey, Marty! The bastard expelled me!" Marty kept jogging, his eyes straight ahead. Fred Brompton yelled even louder, "Marty, you deaf or something? I've been kicked out!"

Fred moved onto the court and stood in Marty's path. Increasing his speed, the older Brompton straight-armed his brother—a massive shove, with the heel of his hand smashing into Fred's nose. Stunned as much by his brother's attack as by the fierce pain, Fred fell against the wall and slid down until he sat on the gym floor, blood streaming from his nose.

Marty Brompton stopped jogging and stood over his brother. "You goddamn meathead!" he said as he raised his fist and then dropped it. "Didn't I tell you to lay the whole thing on Howes and Maguire if it came to that?"

"I couldn't," Fred Brompton whined, staring at the floor. "It all happened so fast. I didn't have a chance. What the hell did you hit me for?"

"For screwing up. From now on, I'm going to be known as the brother of that punk who got expelled. It's like living in the same house with somebody who's got leprosy."

"Is there anything we can *do*?" Fred wailed, holding a handkerchief to his nose. "Couldn't dad—"

"No, he wouldn't. You know that," Marty said. "How many times have you heard him say, 'You've made your own pigsty, now wallow in it!'"

"Lots of times." Fred was near tears.

"No," Marty said. "There'll be no help from him. And mom will just cry and cry and cry. Jesus, what a mess you've made."

"Would *you* talk to the headmaster?" Fred said as he looked at his brother. "Maybe you could tell him you'd be responsible from now on for my keeping out of trouble?"

"And those other two punks, Howes and Maguire?" Marty asked.

"I'm not tied to them. You said that yourself. Let them figure out their own way to get out of this."

"Well," Marty said, scratching his neck and digging into his ear to pull out some wax. "I guess it couldn't hurt. But you, you meathead, you're coming with me and you're going to be crying and sobbing. And, if necessary, you're going to be on your knees. You'd better be the most repentant sinner in the whole history of the world, or I'll kick the shit out of you."

"Gee, thanks, Marty." The blood from Fred's nose was now on his shirt and pants. "I knew I could count on you."

"Just this once, stupid. And if this doesn't work, I don't know you. You understand? I don't know you."

"What does that mean, for Chrissake?" Fred slowly got to his feet. "What do you mean, you won't know me?"

"If this doesn't work, if you're still going to be expelled," Marty Brompton said, "I don't know you anymore. I can't be clearer than that. I had a brother once, and he died somewhere. In a stampede of wild pigs, we heard. Terrible accident."

"You really *would* do that, wouldn't you?" Fred banged his head with his hand. "All you care about is yourself. You don't give a damn about what happens to me."

"Listen, punk, would you give a damn about somebody who shook down little kids, and then got caught?"

"I'd stand up for *you*, no matter what you did," Fred said.

"No, you wouldn't," Marty said, as he dug some wax out of his other ear. "You're for Number One, I'm for Number One. That's the way the world goes. Unfortunately you have the same last name as I do, and that's why I'm going to try to fix things up. But don't kid yourself, punk. I don't stay with losers. Not for long, I don't."

Marty walked into the locker room and Fred began to sob, much to his own disgust.

By noontime, news of the expulsions had spread throughout the school. In the teachers' lounge, Mr. Kozodoy, as he usually did when disappointed, put two extra teaspoonsful of sugar in his coffee.

"I don't hear any confession of error," Miss Saperstein said as she looked up from her newspaper.

"Yes, I was wrong about Sam's being involved in the stealing," Mr. Kozodoy admitted gloomily. "But I am not wrong about the basic nature of the boy. He is essentially uncontrollable and therefore sets a very bad example for the other boys."

"He is no such thing," Miss Sullivan said from the doorway. "I sometimes wish that some of Sam's liveliness could be transfused into some of our duller boys. I don't mean 'dull' intellectually. Some of them are quite bright. Actually, I suppose I mean 'passive' rather than 'dull.' They sit and sit and listen and listen, they do all their homework and pass their exams, but somehow they are so *boring*. I wish we had more Sams around here."

"Bite your tongue," said Miss Saperstein, but she was smiling. "I was very pleased it turned out that Sam wasn't involved in the stealing. I must say, though, that this whole affair is most disturbing. It was a terrible thing those boys did, and it seems to me that expelling them is hardly the way to change them. It'll just make them worse."

"Exactly," Mr. Kozodoy said. "And let us suppose that Sam *had* been proved guilty. Can you imagine the headmaster expelling his own son?"

"I certainly can," Miss Sullivan said. "Mr. Davidson is the kind of person who would reject a huge settlement in an accident case because he really hadn't been injured that much. It's a noble way to be, but it's also rather intimidating to us lesser mortals."

"I think you overestimate the headmaster when it comes to his own flesh and blood," Mr. Kozodoy said. "In any case, I am drawing up a letter asking the headmaster to reconsider these expulsions. Punishment is one thing, but this is overkill. I have worked with those three boys, and they are not irredeemably wicked."

"Except Sam," Miss Sullivan said frostily.

"Even *he* could be worked with," Mr. Kozodoy said, "if he were the only boy in the class and the teacher were aspiring to sainthood."

"I'll sign that letter," said Miss Saperstein, rising and looking at her watch. "Expelling any boy is a copout. If he's that bad, *we* have failed."

"The hell we have!" Miss Sullivan banged down her coffee cup. "What a lot of nonsense. We are not psychiatrists, we certainly are not saints, and it is absurd to pretend that we can save all children's souls. What those three boys did was despicable. I couldn't look at any one of them now without wanting to retch. This place is a whole lot better without them. Let somebody else try to rehabilitate those weasels. I get paid to teach."

"Have you no compassion?" Mr. Kozodoy asked with all the earnestness he could muster.

"A good deal more than you have," Miss Sullivan snapped. "I see what you're doing. If the headmaster comes out of this as some kind of heartless disciplinarian, why there might be a call for a new headmaster—the suddenly humanitarian Kozodoy."

"Let us see," Mr. Kozodoy said with a wintry smile. "Let us see what the parents think."

16

"I don't care what you say," Liz Davidson said angrily as she passed the salad to her husband. "That's a lousy thing Kozodoy is doing—circulating that letter saying you ought to reconsider expelling those three louts. Are you just going to sit there and let him undermine you?"

Mr. Davidson smiled. "It's a free country. I wouldn't want to interfere with that dedicated man's right to freedom of expression. I also happen to know that he's only been able to get about a dozen signatures on that fool letter. And," he added contentedly, "it will be a distinct pleasure to increase Mr. Kozodoy's teaching load next term."

"Well, I wouldn't stand for it for one minute," his wife persisted. Sam looked from one parent to the other as if he were watching a tennis match.

"And then you would find yourself in one hell of a mess." The headmaster reached for the bread. "The true mark of successful authority is the ability to make and execute a decision and *then* allow for all the debate anybody wants. If I were to try to muzzle Kozodoy, it would look as if I were insecure about having expelled those three louts, as you put it. And once teachers and children pick up the scent of fear in a headmaster, he's had it."

"Maybe you're right," Liz Davidson said. "But I do despise that man, even if I happen to agree with him in this case."

The headmaster's eyebrows went up. "Really?"

"Yes, I've been thinking about it and, in a way, your throwing those boys out does reflect rather badly on the school and on you. They've been there since the first grade and if they have rotten characters, which they do, why didn't you and your fine, hand-picked faculty find that out a long time ago? And once you finally *do* find out, you just wash your hands of them. It seems to me that with all the tuition you charge, you should have done better than that."

"Pass the potatoes," Sam said and then caught his father's eye. "Please."

"I would never say any of this to anybody else, you understand," the headmaster's wife went on. "I wouldn't give that worm Kozodoy the satisfaction. Besides, I don't want you to get fired."

"I'm touched by your loyalty." Mr. Davidson's voice had a chill in it. "Actually," his tone softened, "we did fail with those three, and that does bother me. It bothers me a lot. This whole thing has been very troubling. I can't get that little fourth-grader out of my mind. Imagine, a ten-year-old telling me that school isn't a safe place for him, and being quite right."

"That Steve Gorman's a good kid," Sam said as he speared a lamb chop halfway across the table.

"Yes, he is," his father said. "And so are you."

Sam looked up from his plate a little warily.

"Let me put this on the record, Sam," Mr. Davidson said. "I never believed Rawlins' story. I know you too well to have believed it. But I had to be fair and impartial, and by my handling it that way and letting all the facts come out, you were completely cleared— as I knew you would be."

"Lucky for you that it did work out that way," Liz Davidson said to her husband.

Sam grinned. "I heard you yelling at dad last night. You couldn't *never* speak to him. You couldn't *never* speak to nobody."

"Double negative," his mother said.

"You like to talk," Sam continued, "more than anybody I know."

"You watch it," his mother said, smiling.

"I'm just telling the truth," Sam said as he cut his meat. "No disrespect."

"Carl," Liz Davidson said, "what about those three boys? Shouldn't they be given another chance?"

"I've thought about it," the headmaster answered, "but if a school isn't going to fall apart, there are certain kinds of wholly unacceptable behavior that have to be dealt with instantly and drastically. At Alcott, there is no second chance for any student caught *selling* drugs to another student. If a student is caught with a small amount of grass on him, I do give him a second chance. But selling dope cannot be tolerated, and expulsion for that offense has worked as a deterrent. Since I did that to the Roehrlich boy two years ago, there have been no other instances of drug selling in the school."

"As far as you know," his wife interrupted.

"I can't make myself invisible and police the whole school all the time. 'As far as I know' is the best I can do. Anyway, extortion is certainly at least as serious as trafficking in drugs. In both cases, you're faced with the most fundamental responsibility any school has—the physical and moral protection of its students. Whoever is to be blamed for Brompton, Howes, and Maguire growing up twisted—and I have to accept part of that blame—I simply cannot allow the rest of the students to continue to be exposed to their foul presence. Furthermore, and this is my main point, I don't think we'll see any more extortion at Alcott for a long time. That's the difference, so far as deterrence is concerned, between suspension and expulsion."

"You think you'll be fired because of that letter Mr. Kozodoy is passing around about those bastards?" Sam asked.

"No. And watch your language. There are only a few teachers and parents who have the weird and quite destructive notion that youngsters should not be held responsible for their acts. Kozodoy himself doesn't believe that. He's only doing this as a political tactic to weaken my authority at Alcott, and it won't work. But tell me, Sam, what do *you* think about the expulsions? You seldom deprive us of your opinions about anything. Would you have done what I did?"

"You were too soft," Sam said. "They should have

been whipped in front of the whole school. Like in that old movie about Captain Bligh."

"You're not serious?" his mother asked.

"How many lashes?" said his father, trying to appear judicial.

"Oh, about a hundred apiece. And after they were whipped, a stake should have been driven into each of their hearts."

"My God!" Sam's mother said, obviously startled. "You don't really mean any of that."

Sam laughed. "I was just enjoying myself," he said. "I don't think that throwing them out of Alcott is much of a punishment, though. It's more like a present."

"That's enough of that," his father said.

"O.K.," Sam said, "but what about my transferring to another school? Let me at least try it. If it doesn't work out, I can always come back."

"I'm not so sure about that," the headmaster answered, deadpan. "We'd have to review your qualifications."

"Well, if I wanted to come back, I guess I'd have to ask the headmaster at Alcott to write me a letter of recommendation."

"The headmaster's wife would write it," Liz Davidson said, smiling, "and he'd sign it."

Sam, well pleased with himself, took another lamb chop.

17

"Why aren't your parents here?" the head-master asked the two Bromptons as they stood in front of him the following morning. "I asked them to come."

"Well, sir," Marty Brompton said, "they don't really understand what this is all about. I mean, they just won't listen to Fred's side. They're pretty strict, you know."

Fred was rubbing his eyes with his handkerchief, working himself up to start bawling.

"What *is* Fred's side?" The headmaster stared at Marty as Fred tried a few whimpers.

"Well, sir, I hate to say this, sir, but Fred got in with some bad guys. God knows I tried to warn him, but he has this loyalty thing, sir, about his friends, and he sort of just went along with this business, sir, but it wasn't his idea. You see, it was Howes and Maguire who thought it up and, like I said, Fred went along, but he also thought, sir, that by his being along, he could prevent it from getting serious, sir, by keeping Howes and Maguire from losing their heads, sir, and he really did the best he could, and it's because of him, sir, that nobody was really roughed up, sir, even though maybe one of them might have said he was, but if that's so, sir, it must have happened before Fred could stop it. Right, Fred?"

The younger Brompton, taking deep breaths as a warm-up to heavy sighing, nodded his head and pushed some tears out as he did so.

"Are you saying," the headmaster asked, "that while it is fitting for Howes and Maguire to be expelled, your brother should be treated more lightly?"

Marty put his arm around his brother's shoulders. "Sir, it's not for me to tell you what to do about those two, but I think Fred here has more than learned his lesson, and for the rest of his time at Alcott, he'll make you proud of him, sir, he really will."

Fred nodded again, his chin meeting his chest.

"Do either of you have anything else to say?" the headmaster asked.

"No, sir," Marty said. "Except that, well, sir, I don't quite know how to say this, but if in some small way, I've brought some credit to Alcott by being part of the great team we have, sir, unbeaten for a year and a half, as you know, sir, well, maybe I can ask, sir, that some of that credit be transferred to Fred, I mean—"

"Yes, what *do* you mean?" the headmaster asked caustically.

"Well, sir, I've worked hard, very hard, for the school, sir, and—"

"And you want to share the rewards with your stray brother here, although I had foolishly thought that playing as well as you can is its own reward."

"Oh, I don't mean that the honor of being on the team isn't enough, sir, isn't more than enough. It's just that, well, sir, the Brompton name has meant something to the school, and if Fred here can get just one more chance, why, sir, he'll live up to that name."

"He wouldn't have much of a distance to go to live up to the name," the headmaster said, "in view, of your performance here this morning."

"Sir?" Marty Brompton said in confusion and some alarm.

"First of all," the headmaster began, "you are not so much your brother's keeper as you are your brother's liar. Not that he needs much help in that department. I have talked to Howes and Maguire and also to the boys who were victimized by them and by your brother. There is total agreement on the fact that your brother, far from being a reluctant member of this trio of thugs, was actually its enthusiastic leader."

"They're lying, sir!" Fred Brompton howled. "They're lying!" He continued to shout as he fell on his knees. "Please, sir, don't let their lies ruin my life!"

"For God's sake, get up!" the headmaster said. "Have you no self-respect left at all? No, I don't suppose you have, but I would appreciate it if you kept that mucus of yours off the carpet."

Marty grabbed his younger brother by the collar and yanked him up.

"You have come to me under several pretenses," the headmaster said to Marty. "One is that your brother is decidedly less guilty than his two cohorts and that, in fact, he served to make their vicious sport less harsh. That is an outright lie."

"But, sir—" Marty Brompton tried to interrupt.

"Second," the headmaster continued, "you claim that this school owes you something for your having made the football team. And rather than hoard this reward all for yourself, you are so selfless, so generous, that you wish to have a portion of it transferred to your pathetically innocent, though easily misled brother."

"Sir, that's not fair—" Marty Brompton again tried to interrupt.

"Third," the headmaster cut him off, "you pretend to come here as a seeker of justice, or at least clemency, for your brother, when what is *really* bothering you is that since both of you have the same last name, some of the mud he has picked up will rub off on you. In addition, you are perfectly willing to shunt off blame from your brother to his co-conspirators. I must say that this whole wretched performance has tempted me to—"

Fred Brompton raised his head in wholly illogical hope.

"—change my mind about Howes and Maguire, although I shall not. I have, however, changed my mind about you." The headmaster looked directly at Marty. "I have misread you through the years. I had no idea of how dishonest, how much of a fraud you are."

"You're calling me a *fraud?*" Marty roared as if in pain.

"Your hearing is excellent," the headmaster said. "Yes, you are a fraud, and worse. You tried to throw all the blame on Howes and Maguire and that is disgusting."

"Now, listen here—" Marty's face was reddening.

"Listen here, *sir*," the headmaster emphasized. "You seemed to have had a goodly supply of 'sirs' before. Have you run out of them?"

"You've got no right to call me all those names," Marty said. "I'm not the one who did anything wrong. *He's* the one." Marty shoved an elbow into his brother's side."

"I am beginning to see," the headmaster said, "who your younger brother's model has been."

Marty Brompton shook his head as if a baseball bat had just landed on it. "Damn it, sir, I didn't come up here to get into any trouble."

"Nonetheless, you have."

"What *is* this?" Marty shouted. "What have I done wrong? I was just trying to help my brother."

The headmaster rose. "Perhaps your hearing isn't as good as I thought. But I shall not repeat myself. I shall, however, keep a very close watch on you for the remainder of your last year here."

Marty Brompton was still stunned. "I have a good record, I never got into any trouble. I'm a good guy." He looked beseechingly at the headmaster. "Ask the coach what a good guy I am." All of a sudden, Marty's eyes widened. "Hey, wait a minute! Is any of this going to get on—I mean, what are you going to write about me when you send my records to the colleges I've applied to?"

"I'm not sure yet," the headmaster said. "I'll have to think about that very carefully."

"Oh, wow!" Marty Brompton banged a fist hard against his thigh and winced. "Oh, wow, this is what you get for trying to help out your own brother. Oh, wow!"

"Now that you have taken to howling," the headmaster said, "I would suggest you indulge in that peculiar avocation outside this office."

"Does this mean I'm still expelled?" asked Fred Brompton, wiping his eyes.

"You do have problems of comprehension," the headmaster said, motioning toward the door. "I trust your next school will be able to help you with them."

Outside the headmaster's office, the two brothers walked in silence along the corridor.

"What went wrong, Marty?" Fred finally asked. "And when did it begin to go wrong?"

"When you were born, you goddamn punk," Marty Brompton spat out. "That's when it began to go wrong."

Every day for a week, Marty Brompton had stopped at the bulletin board diagonally across the corridor from the headmaster's office. And every day, as Marty pretended to be intensely interested in each notice on the board, he would see out of the corner of his eye that the headmaster's secretary was at her desk. But this morning, she was not there.

Trying to appear casual while his heart was pounding, Marty slowly crossed the hall and walked into the headmaster's outer office. Finding the inner office also empty, he looked out into the empty corridor and then went into the inner office, closed the door, and examined the labels on the filing cabinets that lined one wall. He stopped at a label marked *Seniors/College,* opened the file cabinet, and located a manila folder with his name on it. Glancing back into the outer office, he opened the folder and read:

> Martin Brompton is an outstanding athlete. His academic work is of average quality, but that is less an index of his potential, I believe, than it is a reflection of his preference for athletics over school work. He has never let his grades fall to the point at which he would have been ineligible for athletics; but on the other hand, he has never made the honors list.
>
> Until this year, I had considered Martin Brompton to be of good character. I now have my doubts. If you are considering his application seriously, I would appreciate your telephoning me, as I do not want to set whatever reservations I have about this young man on paper, since it would then become part of his permanent school record. I am troubled at having to write this, particularly since only one incident led to my reassessment of his character, but it was sufficiently grave to warrant some discussion.
>
> I am a believer in the perfectibility of man, and especially of boys, and thus I do not wish to do this young man an injustice. But I would not be fulfilling my obligation of candor to you if I were to make no mention

at all of the change in my judgment of him. Let me emphasize that I do not want to foreclose his college future. Your college, because of the small size of the student body, and the consequent close attention each student receives, may well be the best place for him. So please do not hesitate to call.

Sincerely,
Carl Davidson
Headmaster

Marty stared at the manila folder in his hand. "I should tear this goddamn thing up," he muttered, "but he'd know right away who did it." He placed the folder back in the file cabinet and closed it. "Well, thanks a lot." He looked at the headmaster's desk. "Thanks a whole hell of a lot. You'd think I'd murdered the school nurse or something."

He left the inner office, heard steps in the corridor, and quickly sat down in one of the chairs across the room from the secretary's desk.

"Do you have an appointment?" she said, coming in the door.

"Not really. I just thought I'd take a chance that the headmaster would have time to see me."

"I'm afraid that he won't be back this afternoon. But I can make an appointment for tomorrow."

"No, thanks," Marty said over his shoulder as he walked to the door. "It wasn't all that important, and I guess I know the answer anyway."

18

It was early June, seven months later, and Sam, Blake, and Benjy were standing on the sidewalk near the school. There was a quarter of an hour until classes began.

"I saw that bastard Fred Brompton on the subway yesterday," Benjy said. "He looked right through me. But then, I looked right through him. Where is he now, do you know? And those other guys?"

"My father says," Sam answered, "that the three of them got into some dumb private school that accepts anybody so long as he's breathing and his parents have the money to pay the tuition. I'm not sure he has to be breathing."

"It's a funny thing," Blake said, "how the school has quieted down since all that happened. I mean, I walk by the detention room some afternoons and there's only a couple of guys there."

"Simple," Benjy said. "You see an explosion in the news on television, with people spread all around the place, and you're glad you weren't in it, right? Same thing when somebody gets thrown out of a school. You're so glad it wasn't you, whether you like the place or not, that you don't get into trouble—for a while anyway."

"Yeah," Blake said, "I guess nothing makes you appreciate a place more than seeing somebody else get kicked out of it. Like the club I'm in. We had a dude who was doing all kinds of crazy things and getting some of the smaller fellows into his craziness. So we kicked him the hell out. Man, now he'd pay all he has to get back in. But no way. And the little fellows, they've cooled right down. More or less. There's a couple of them need to be kicked in the ass every once in a while."

"It is funny," Sam said. "I almost want to stay here now. I dunno. I feel a little better about the place, but—"

"But what?" Benjy asked.

"I really want to try school somewhere else. I think I do, anyway. I want to know what it's like to be in a school where the headmaster is just the headmaster, you know. I think I'd be better off that way. I'd be just another kid."

"I don't see anybody here asking for your autograph," Blake said.

"You know what I mean." Sam threw a fake punch at Blake. "No, I guess you don't. Nobody could but me. Anyway, I'm gonna try it."

"See you after school," Benjy said rather sadly as he went up the steps.

"Make that at home," Sam called after him. "I only have a couple hours of classes today because I'm going to the graduation."

"What for?" Blake asked.

"Well, it *is* my last year here," Sam said, "and I thought I'd take a look at what it's like if you go all the way."

"You can always change your mind about leaving, you know," Benjy said. "I mean, we sure don't want you to leave."

Blake nodded. "Yeah, a lot of fun will go out of this place. Every school needs a nut."

"Jees," Sam said, "that's some way to say good-bye."

"There are worse ways," Blake said with a smile.

"I'll miss you guys, too," Sam said.

Fat Jake, eyes straight ahead, came up the stairs and passed the three friends without acknowledgment.

"Boy," Benjy said, "that guy must like staying mad. It's been months since the truck ran over his lunch box."

"Hey, Jake," Sam shouted, "you lost something!" Jake turned around.

"Just wanted to see if you'd gone deaf, too," Sam said, "because your eyesight's none too good."

"One day," Jake said, "one day I'm going to get you guys. One at a time. First one of you goes, and the other two know they haven't much time left."

"I saw that movie on television last week," Blake said. "So I know all your moves. You come after me, fat boy, and that'll be the end of you. You will be totaled. Gone. Just a hunk of pork."

"Come on." Sam pulled Blake's coat sleeve. "Enough's enough. He really did like that lunch box, you know."

"Yeah, well I don't like anybody walking right by me as if I'm not there," Blake said. "You hear that, fat boy?"

Fat Jake squinted. "Oh, yes, *there* you are. It's very hard to see you when the sun's not out."

"You goddamn—"

Jake jumped and ran down the hall with Blake sprinting after him.

"Stop! Stop!" Mr. Kozodoy came out of his room. "Both of you—stop this instant."

Jake turned around, still running, and put himself behind Mr. Kozodoy as Blake waved a fist at him.

"What is this all about?" the teacher said wearily.

"They were just fooling around." Sam moved next to Blake.

"Yeah," Benjy said. "They were just having a race."

"I don't believe it," Mr. Kozodoy scowled. "I don't believe one word of it. And you," he pointed to Sam, "I bet you were behind it, whatever it is."

"What are you going to do without me next year, Mr. Kozodoy?" Sam said. "Who are you going to blame for everything?"

"My boy, I plan to celebrate your leavetaking as a precious personal holiday. Each year, on that day, I shall give special thanks that you are no longer here."

"He's going away? He's going away?" Jake repeated anxiously. "Then tell him to give me back those baseball cards he stole last winter."

"Oh, Christ, I don't know anything about your cards." Sam shook his head. "You see," Sam said to

Benjy and Blake, "that's another reason I want to get out of here. In the new school, I'll be starting clean. Nobody will know anything about me or think they know anything about me. It'll be like a new life, you know."

"They will know a good deal more than they want to know about you soon enough," Mr. Kozodoy intoned. "A leopard never changes his spots."

"Boy, I really appreciate that, Mr. Kozodoy," Sam said. "It's just like you to give me something warm and friendly to remember you by."

Blake and Benjy snickered.

"Amuse yourselves while you may." Mr. Kozodoy turned to Blake and Benjy. "Because I will be in charge of your homeroom next year. It would be wise for you to spend your summer reflecting on that."

Mr. Kozodoy walked on with Jake, who turned around and thumbed his nose.

"You got something to think about this summer too, fat boy," Blake pointed at Jake.

"I sure am going to miss all this," Sam said. "I really am."

Two hours later, in the school auditorium, the choir had sung its required pieces. The guest speaker, a congressman, had told the seniors, sitting stiffly on the stage, that the future of the country was in their hands. ("God help us all," Mr. Kozodoy had muttered.) And now the headmaster rose.

In the twelfth row, Sam sat next to the aisle, and looked around at everyone waiting for his father to speak.

"Now there's a man who knows how to make a

school hum," the man in front of Sam said to the woman beside him.

They ought to see him at home, Sam thought, yelling for mom whenever anything happens to the lights or the television gets blurry or the toilet overflows. Sam had often heard his mother tell his father, "It's a wonder that you can tie your shoelaces by yourself."

But I guess he is a pretty good headmaster. Sam looked at his father, who was calm and unmistakably in command onstage. I mean, Sam was thinking, he really does take charge when he has to. Like that mess about the stealing. And he's fair in school, even to his own son, not like he is at home when I get yelled at sometimes just for breathing. The best thing he ever said to me was when he finally told me he knew I couldn't have done what that bastard Rawlins said I did.

Yeah, Sam looked at the stage, there are worse fathers you could have. A lot worse.

Sam turned to his mother. "Is dad going to make a long speech?"

"He intended to, but I finally convinced him last night, as I have every June, that he is not the reason all these people are here. Next year I'm going to start working on him to do without the guest speaker. It's the brief, simple ceremony that stays in people's minds."

Sam looked at the stage. "Hey," he whispered anxiously. "Where's dad's speech? Did he forget it?"

"Your father prides himself on never speaking from notes. He says that if you know what you want to say and your mind is clear, you don't need notes.

That's why he usually speaks so long. There's never a last page to stop him. Well, here he goes."

"I have a special treat for you," the headmaster said, smiling. "I will forgo any preface to the granting of diplomas except to say that this is a class of which we are particularly proud."

"Does he say that every year?" Sam whispered.

"Yes," his mother answered.

The headmaster glanced at the head of the upper school standing next to him in front of a small table on which the diplomas had been arranged. The head of the upper school handed the headmaster the first diploma.

"Is that *all* he's going to say?" Sam was disappointed.

"My God, I believe it is," his mother said. "An old dog *can* learn new tricks."

As each boy came forward to receive his diploma, the headmaster shook his hand warmly. Then the student, smiling broadly, returned to his seat. A few looked at their diplomas with some disbelief.

"It's a hard school, a very hard school," Sam heard a woman behind him saying. "But when they get out of here, they usually find the first year of college a breeze."

"It's too hard, if you ask me," another woman responded. "He makes them work so hard they scarcely have a chance to be in touch with their feelings."

"Young people today have entirely too many feelings as it is, if you ask *me*," the first woman said.

As his father got to the Bs, Sam leaned forward,

focusing on Marty Brompton. Marty was sitting bolt upright, his face expressionless.

"Martin Brompton," the headmaster announced.

Brompton got up quickly and walked across the stage. The headmaster held out his hand. Brompton stopped in front of the headmaster, looked past him at the wall, and kept his hands at his side.

There were gasps from the audience. "Did you see that? Did you see that?" one of the talkative women behind Sam said. "How awful! How rude!"

On stage, the headmaster, surprised into brief embarrassment, dropped his hand, turned, and took Brompton's diploma from the head of the upper school. He turned back to hand it to Brompton, but Brompton grabbed the diploma from the headmaster's hand, swung around, and marched briskly back to his seat, where again he sat without expression.

"That bastard," Sam said.

"You watch your language," his mother whispered, and then stared coldly at Brompton, who was meeting no one's eyes. "That son-of-a-bitch," she muttered.

Sam's eyebrows lifted and he was about to say something to his mother, but seeing the fury in her face, he decided to keep quiet.

Carl Davidson shrugged his shoulders and announced the recipient of the next diploma, whom he greeted with a smile and a handshake.

For a while, the murmuring in the audience continued, but gradually it stopped. The headmaster, appearing to be not in the least ruffled, continued handing out the diplomas. The last handshake and the last roll of parchment having been given, the choir began to sing the school song, "Arise, Ye Sons of Alcott."

Two by two, the seniors left the stage and walked up the aisle toward the back of the auditorium. Sam watched the procession intently and bit his lips. Just as Marty Brompton was about to pass his row, Sam, gazing innocently at the stage, stuck his foot out into the aisle.

Brompton, who had been staring straight ahead, tripped and landed heavily in the laps of two astonished older women in the row behind Sam.

"Good gracious, young man, do you take drugs?" one of the women, with white hair, said indignantly. Brompton struggled to get to his feet without putting his hands on her or on the other woman.

"You lummox!" said the white-haired woman as she tried to push Brompton away.

A senior in the procession behind Brompton put his hands under Brompton's shoulders and, tugging mightily, managed to drag him off and dump him in the aisle. There were snorts of laughter from the surrounding rows of parents and children, and the seniors up ahead looked back at the commotion with wide grins on their faces.

Scrambling to his feet, a red-faced Marty Brompton looked behind him and his eyes met Sam's. Sam nodded politely.

Brompton clenched his hands, snarled, "Crummy father, crummy son," and plodded up the aisle.

Looking to the stage again, Sam caught his father's eye. He was not entirely sure, but it did seem to him that his father, just barely, winked at him.